Resounding praise for

and he[r] ...ysteries

...World

"**A** substance and depth not usually associated with cozy mysteries . . . Nothing I've read in Christie comes close."

Los Angeles Times

"**C**hurchill's spare yet eloquent prose fits perfectly with an era that eschews waste of any kind. The nice mix of Depression history and cozy ambience is reminiscent of a Preston Sturges film."

Booklist

"**C**hurchill's stories are written to amuse and entertain, and this they do in abundace."

Chicago Sun-Times

"**[Her]** dialogue is as familiar as the gossip at a kitchen coffee klatch."

Cleveland Plain Dealer

"**C**hurchill combines historical atmosphere with plucky characterizations and a palatable dose of social responsibility. . . . [She] will leave you feeling a little bit better about human nature."

Washington Post Book World

Books by Jill Churchill

Grace and Favor Series
WHO'S SORRY NOW?
IT HAD TO BE YOU
LOVE FOR SALE
IN THE STILL OF THE NIGHT
ANYTHING GOES

Jane Jeffry Series
A MIDSUMMER NIGHT'S SCREAM
BELL, BOOK, AND SCANDAL
THE HOUSE OF SEVEN MABELS
MULCH ADO ABOUT NOTHING
A GROOM WITH A VIEW
THE MERCHANT OF MENACE
FEAR OF FRYING
WAR AND PEAS
SILENCE OF THE HAMS
FROM HERE TO PATERNITY
A KNIFE TO REMEMBER
THE CLASS MENAGERIE
A QUICHE BEFORE DYING
A FAREWELL TO YARNS
GRIME AND PUNISHMENT

Forthcoming
THE ACCIDENTAL FLORIST

WHO'S SORRY NOW?

A GRACE & FAVOR MYSTERY

JILL CHURCHILL

AVON BOOKS
An Imprint of HarperCollins*Publishers*

Author's Note

"Who's Sorry Now" was written and composed in 1923 by Burt Kalmar, Harry Ruby, and Ted Snyder.

This book is a work of fiction. The characters, incidents and dialogue are drawn from the author's imagination and are not to be construed as real. Any resemblance to actual events or persons, living or dead, is entirely coincidental.

AVON BOOKS
An Imprint of HarperCollins*Publishers*
10 East 53rd Street
New York, New York 10022-5299

ISBN-13: 978-0-06-073460-2
ISBN: 0-06-073460-4
www.avonmystery.com

First Avon Books paperback printing: November 2006
First William Morrow hardcover printing: December 2005

Printed in the U.S.A.

10 9 8 7 6 5 4 3 2 1

CHAPTER ONE

Monday, April 17, 1933

ROBERT BREWSTER WAS WAITING around the train station in Voorburg-on-Hudson for a box of books he'd ordered for his sister Lily's next birthday. A week ago, he'd sneaked away to New York City with a list the comely town librarian had given him. Miss Philomena Exley knew Lily's reading habits and favorite authors. He'd been told that two of the author choices she'd enjoyed had new books coming out the end of the week if he'd care to wait for just one package to be shipped by train to Voorburg.

Since he was doing this much earlier than necessary, which was not the way he normally treated birthdays, Robert didn't mind. Mostly, he frantically picked up some silly trinket at the last minute, and offered to pay Lily's way to a talkie. But getting to speak at length with Miss Exley was a rare treat.

Since there was no longer a post office in Voorburg because it burned down years ago, the incoming mail and packages were in bags at the train station and the residents had to rummage through the bags to fish out what they'd received.

There was a porter who hung around the station, helping with luggage and living on the tips, which must have been meager in these hard times. Edwin McBride had been at the Bonus March and heard Jack Summer, the editor of the *Voorburg Times,* talk about Voorburg. It had sounded like a nice town so he'd settled there. "A box for you, Mr. Brewster," McBride said. "Really heavy."

Robert tipped him fifty cents, which was probably more than McBride normally made in a week, and set the box down on a bench, to figure out where to hide it from Lily. As he was doing so, a familiar Voorburg resident stepped off the last car, which was for passengers. She was Sara Smithson, a young widow who had inherited a lot of rental property from her husband. She looked exhausted as she gestured for Mr. McBride to help her with her enormous suitcase, then a large trunk. The trunk was followed by an older man, who needed help down the steep steps.

Robert approached her. "May I help you and this gentleman?"

"Oh, Mr. Brewster, how nice of you. It's been such a long hard trip."

"From where?" Robert asked, not that it was any of his business.

She didn't mind telling him. "Clear from Berlin, Germany."

She pushed back her hair, which was straggling loose from under her hat.

"I went to fetch my grandfather." She put her hand on the old man's arm and glanced at Robert. "This nice man, Mr. Brewster, is going to help us with our belongings."

The old man took Robert's hand, and introduced himself. "Schneidermeister Kurtz."

"Grandpa, say it in English," Mrs. Smithson said with a hint of irritation. "I've told you not many people here know German."

He patted his granddaughter's arm and with a smile, said, "Yes, you have, sweeting. I'm Master Tailor Kurtz. My granddaughter came to rescue me from the Nazis." Robert was surprised at how well the old man spoke English. Only the faintest hint of German accent.

"Are you Jewish, then?" Robert asked.

"No, Catholic," he said. "But once I went with a friend to a Communist meeting. We all had to sign our names and addresses in a ledger so we'd get a notice of the time and place of the next meeting. The Nazis hate Communists as much as Jews. I feared someone would turn me in if they found the ledger."

It took both Robert and McBride to thrust Mr. Kurtz's trunk and Mrs. Smithson's big suitcase into the back of Robert's butter-yellow Duesenberg.

"What a fine car this is," Mr. Kurtz said. "You must be very wealthy to have one."

"Grandpa! That's rude," Mrs. Smithson said.

"I don't mind at all," Robert said. "I inherited it from a great-uncle I didn't even remember. My sister and I are as poor as everyone else in town. Mrs. Smithson, where am I taking you and your grandfather?"

"I live next door to Miss Jurgen. Do you know her house?"

"I do. My sister Lily takes sewing lessons from her."

"I know. I take lessons at the same time she does. But it's not sewing. It's graphing patterns for embroidery and needlepoint. But we need to drop off Grandpa's trunk first."

"Where?"

"That little empty shop across from the courthouse that used to be a bookstore before the tenant and his family took off for California. My late husband owned it."

Robert pulled up in front of the building and said, "We're going to have to have some help with this trunk. Your grandfather can't endanger his hands or back trying to carry it. It's very heavy. I'll go and see if the newspaper editor, Jack Summer, can help me."

"I hate putting so many people to all this trouble."

"It's no trouble at all. And you can do me a favor. Hide this box of books in your house until my sister's birthday, if you would."

"Small payment for all you've done," she said, fishing in her handbag for the keys to the building.

Robert and Jack were back in minutes. "How can a trunk be so darned heavy?" Jack asked.

"Mr. Kurtz is a tailor," Robert explained. "A Master Tailor, in fact. He must have his sewing machine and all his shears, scissors, and threads in it. Probably lots of fabrics as well."

They were both out of breath by the time they'd hoisted it up the two steps to the shop. They could hear voices from the floor above, where there were probably living quarters.

"In English, Grandpa," came Mrs. Smithson's voice.

"But you know German, too."

"Not very well, Grandpa, and I don't speak it anymore. You shouldn't either. German speakers aren't very well liked in America these days."

She came down the stairs and shook hands with both Robert and Jack and thanked them again. "He's an old man and stuck in his ways. I guess he's entitled to be, but it's not wise to speak German in the States today."

She said to Robert and Jack, "Just leave the trunk here

in the middle of the room. Grandpa can sort out where to put his professional objects and take his clothing and personal things upstairs later."

"Mrs. Smithson, could I interview your grandfather when he's settled in?" Jack Summer asked.

"I suppose so. But why?"

"People in town like feeling they know a little about newcomers to town. And it might help him get new customers."

Mrs. Smithson, who was only in her mid-thirties, was looking very tired, haggard, and much older than her years. "That's a good idea. But give us both a few days rest, please. It's been a long, harrowing trip from Berlin to here."

"When did you leave Germany?" Robert asked as he opened the passenger door of the Duesie and helped get her settled in comfortably.

Mrs. Smithson waited until he was behind the wheel and said, "April first."

"Just in time," Robert said and made a relieved whistle. "According to Jack Summer, anyone who isn't a native German couldn't leave the country without the permission of the police after April fourth."

"Good Lord! We made it out in the nick of time! We had to take the train to Le Havre, France, then cross the English Channel in a horrible boat in a storm. In England, we went to Portsmouth to get the ship for New York, and then took the train to here. My grandpa has been away from home for seventeen long days. It's hard on an old man to travel that much."

"It would be hard on anyone," Robert agreed. Mrs. Smithson and her grandfather had probably come over second class. Robert and all his family, in the old "rich" days, always went first class, where they were pampered with champagne, heated towels, an excess of excellent food, and luxurious fresh bedding every day.

Those days were long over. If he had to go to Europe these days, he'd be in steerage or hiding in a lifeboat.

"It was awful," Mrs. Smithson said as they approached her house. "All I want is a good hot bath and a shampoo, and to sleep for ten or eleven hours in my own bed." She paused for a moment as Robert stopped in front of her house. Then she added, "But it was worth it all to get Grandpa back here."

"What do you mean by 'back here'?"

She smiled. "He was born in St. Louis. His father was a brewer and took the family to Germany when Grandpa was only eight years old. So Grandfather is an American, too. Though he couldn't have told the police that. He had no birth certificate. The family spoke German at work, and English at home. That's why he speaks English, albeit with a slight German accent."

Robert insisted on carrying her big suitcase into her house and upstairs. And then he went back to the car to take Lily's books in. "I hope my sister isn't at Miss Jurgen's wondering what's in the box."

"If she asks, tell her the box was mine. And this isn't one of the days she gives lessons anyway. Again, I thank you so much. I simply couldn't have stood taking the only taxi in town. We'd probably have to have waited for ages for the driver to turn up, and he wouldn't have helped with the luggage."

When the birthday books were hidden and Robert was again alone, he checked the deep pocket inside his sport coat for the things he'd bought himself while he was in New York City. The small metal items jingled against each other. He'd have to find somewhere at home to hide them and the little brochure that had come with them. Before he headed home, he went to see Howard Walker, the Voorburg chief of police, at the jail building. Howard spent most of his days working there, but he also had an office in a boardinghouse in town. He had a phone line there and often he took the notes home that he'd made on cases so he could study them in his free time.

"Are you busy?" Robert asked Howard.

"Just tidying up the files for storage on that case a month ago. I'll store them at the bank in Fishkill as I usually do."

"I'm just here to ask you a question. I don't expect you to do anything about it except tell me to whom I should talk."

"About what?" Howard rose from his desk and stretched his aching back.

"The Voorburg mail situation. I was expecting a package and went down to the station to wait for the train. There were three old ladies going through the mailbags from the earlier train. The train was a little late and I overheard them saying things like, 'It looks as if Bernice might have a boyfriend. . . . This envelope is pink and I can feel some beading inside.'

"Another of them was examining someone else's mail and said, 'Here's something from that no-good man who writes to you-know-who. I'm tempted to take it home and throw it away. That man isn't worth her time.'"

"Nosy old women," Howard remarked with distaste.

"Here's my suggestion. See what you think. Edwin McBride, the porter at the train station, only works when someone's seriously traveling. The ones who are just going to New York City for the day don't carry luggage. He doesn't make many tips. I understand the Harbinger boys fixed up that shed behind your old house near the river. Heat and water. That's where he lives, probably for free."

Howard sighed. "Robert, get to the point."

"Couldn't whoever controls the public funds kick in just a little money to give the porter a cheap job sorting the mail between trains? I'm sure the Harbinger boys could make up something with a lot of little boxes or drawers. A sorting structure with names at the bottom of each partition. The Harbingers always have a big supply of surplus wood left over from other jobs. It doesn't need to be pretty. They might contribute the wood, but expect to be paid for their time, which is how it should be."

"Okay. You're making sense. It might put a slight crimp in the gossip mill. But the old ladies could still rummage through other people's sections."

"Not if McBride and the stationmaster keep an eye on them and tell them to use only their own sections. How can I go about this?"

"There are five volunteers who have to vote on the city budget. Three of the five, in rotation, are reelected every other year. But there's no pay, except for the permanent treasurer."

"How often do they meet?"

"I'm not sure. Maybe every six months. But you could ask them to consider this sooner, I suppose."

"Who should I start with?"

"Robert, are you sure you want to turn into a do-gooder? Tattling on old ladies?"

"In this case, I do."

"Okay. Here are the names of the town council members. The treasurer's name is underlined. Peter Winchel is a good man and really cares about the welfare of the citizens. I'd suggest you drop a note at each of their houses. Don't name the ladies you heard though. It would get around town like a rabid dog."

"I don't even know who two of them are. And I've only seen another one as I passed the city dump once."

"Good luck," Howard said. He poured himself another cup of coffee and added, as Robert went out the door, "And watch out for Arnold Wood. He's a nasty person."

Robert was going to ask more but Howard sat back down to file the reports in chronological order. "Let me know what they say. If you want me to look over your letters before you deliver them, I'd be glad to help."

Robert sat in the Duesie thinking over what Howard had suggested; then he returned to the jail.

"What about a petition to gather support for my idea?" he asked. "Getting lots of signatures to present at a meeting, if they call one soon?"

"Even better," Walker agreed. "Now leave me alone."

CHAPTER TWO

AT DINNER THAT EVENING, Robert told the whole household—the Prinneys, Lily, Mimi the maid, and their boarders—Phoebe Twinkle, the town milliner, and Mrs. Tarkington, the principal of the grade school—what he'd seen and heard at the railroad station earlier.

They were all shocked. "I don't receive a lot of letters," Mrs. Tarkington said. "But when I do, I don't want strangers examining them."

"Nor do I," Mr. Prinney said. He was the executor of their great-uncle Horatio's trust and had become a friend and mentor, especially to Lily. "The very idea of considering disposing of a letter to someone else for her own good is appalling and possibly illegal. What can be done about this?"

"I talked to Howard Walker about it and we came to

the conclusion that a petition ought to be presented to the town council members. We'd ask that someone—probably the Harbinger boys—but we won't say that in the petition—could build a piece of furniture that has a whole lot of drawers or boxes with doors, labeled with citizens' names."

"That wouldn't stop the snoops," Lily said.

"It would certainly discourage them," Robert said. "And the stationmaster, who would have it in his line of sight, could tell them to only pick up their own mail and leave other people's mail alone."

Phoebe Twinkle spoke up. "Who would sort it?"

"The porter," Robert said. "Poor McBride makes almost nothing on tips and lives in a shed. I'd like to suggest that he be paid a small salary to sort the mail between trains. But it would have to come out of the town's budget."

"How is the town's budget collected?" Phoebe Twinkle asked.

Mr. Prinney said, "In a number of ways. Small taxes for selling cars and property. Fines leveled against bad drivers, and our own property taxes. It mainly funds the grade school."

"Not nearly well enough," Mrs. Tarkington, the principal of the grade school, piped up.

"If we can't squeeze out a tiny bit of money to pay

McBride for sorting the mail," Lily asked, "couldn't it be provided by Great-uncle Horatio's trust? For the good of the town and as a charitable deduction?"

Mr. Prinney frowned for a moment. "I'm not sure that's a good idea."

"Why not?" Lily asked, very politely. "We're not even asking our farmers in Nebraska, Kansas, Oklahoma, and Colorado to pay their mortgages because of the drought, and are more than making it up on the income from the mortgages on the land in California where the movie companies are making money hand over fist."

"You have a good point there, Lily," Mr. Prinney admitted. He was pleased at how well she was learning about the trust Horatio Brewster had left in his hands to eventually end up controlled by his heirs when the time came to turn it over to them.

"We could donate a small amount anonymously, couldn't we?" Robert asked. "But only if the town council doesn't cough it up. I've written up an explanation of the purpose of a petition to appeal to citizens. I'll read it to you after dinner."

When they'd all settled in the library, with the French doors to the small balcony open so they could enjoy the surprisingly warm evening, only Mimi was missing. She was clearing the table and washing up the dinnerware.

Mrs. Prinney served tea as well as coffee for herself, Lily, Mrs. Tarkington, and Phoebe. Robert and Mr. Prinney stood by the balcony with cigars and glasses of wine. Robert soon put his wineglass down and started reading the explanation of the petition he'd written.

The rest were attentive and approving until he read ". . . this came to my attention when I heard three gossipy old biddies . . ."

There was an uproar of objections. Robert just laughed. "It's not really in the petition. But I will tell people I ask to sign about it. I'll sign the first line. Do the rest of you want to sign it tonight?"

Lily said, "I think our signatures should be scattered throughout instead of in a lump at the beginning. We don't mind your rabble-rousing, but we don't want to give a wrong impression that the only people who care all live here."

"Okeydokey," Robert said as he took a fountain pen out of an inside pocket of his over-the-hill dinner jacket and signed on the first line with a flourish at the end.

When he went upstairs to bed, he looked around for a good place to hide what else he'd bought on his book-buying trip to the city. Mimi cleaned every room ferociously at least twice a week, but as far as Robert knew, she never looked inside drawers or cabinets. So he hid his purchase in the drawer with his shaving and bathing things.

On Tuesday Robert was eager to start getting signatures, but there were a few things he needed to do first. He dropped in at the nasty little house right by the railroad tracks that the chief of police had lived in, then sold to the Harbinger boys.

Harry was there. His younger brother Jim was away—busy fixing somebody's plumbing pipe to the bathtub. Robert explained why he had come to visit. "I'm going to get a petition signed by as many people as I can to put up a big piece of furniture to hold people's mail in slots, drawers, or shelves divided into individual places so people don't have to go through all the mailbags to find their own things."

"Good idea. I don't get much mail, but when I'm waiting for something I've ordered like an unusual piece of plumbing tubing, or a special kind of paintbrush, it's a nuisance to rummage through the bags with everyone else's mail."

"I'm glad you like the idea," Robert said. "Mainly because you and your brother will have to make the sorting furniture. You'll be paid for your time and skills, of course," he said breezily, not knowing if this would come true. If not, he'd have to find the money himself. Or rather, Lily would have to persuade Mr. Prinney to use the estate money.

"Could you manage it with scrap lumber?" Robert asked Harry.

"I have more scrap wood than I know what to do with. Now I have a way to get rid of it." Harry rubbed his hands together and smiled. "I've never taken on a job like this, but it sounds interesting."

While they were talking, Robert was taking in their living quarters. Howard Walker had always hated this house. It was close to the river. It had reeked of mildew. The trains shot by in the small gap between the house and the Hudson River, hooting loudly, making it impossible for Howard to ever get a good night's sleep.

The Harbinger boys had done wonders with the house. The windows had been replaced with smaller ones with thicker glass. There was no longer a smell of rot or mildew. They'd apparently used up some of their scrap wood, adding it to the inside wall that faced the railroad tracks as additional soundproofing. One train raced by while they'd been speaking and neither of them had had to raise their voices.

"This plan we've talked about isn't in the petition," Robert said. "I wanted to keep it as simple as I could." He went on to explain what had led him to take this on, describing the three old women pawing over other people's mail, and one of them even suggesting that they destroy one letter for the recipient's own good.

Harry was shocked. "Do you have a pen? I'll sign it right now. Nobody should be able to destroy other folks' letters or cards."

After he'd signed his name, he said, "I'll start drawing up some plans. I might do two or three and let whoever makes the decision choose."

"Thanks, Harry. I have to get one or two more people to agree about the petition before I start collecting the rest of the signatures."

Robert went back to the train station and asked Mr. Buchanan, the train stationmaster, if they could speak privately.

"Nothing's very private here. But there's not a train for another twenty minutes. Let's stand outside."

"It's about those women I saw pawing through everybody else's letters and cards," Robert said.

Buchanan nodded. "It's disgraceful, isn't it? Nosy old things."

"Right," Robert said, glad to hear that Buchanan agreed.

He handed the petition to Buchanan, who looked it over and had questions. "Who's going to build it? Who's going to sort it?" Are the drawers or boxes going to have a combination lock?"

Robert paused before replying. "I hadn't thought of locks. I'll tell the Harbinger boys to put hardware on and those who want to can buy a lock."

"But lots of people don't come in every day for their mail. Who will put the mail in the boxes without knowing the combination?"

Robert was embarrassed to admit he hadn't thought of that either. "But I did think about who would sort. I think the city fathers should pay Mr. McBride to sort it."

Robert was suddenly discouraged by his plan. Other people he would be approaching would ask the same questions, and probably others he hadn't thought of. He decided to consult with the residents of Grace and Favor for what else he might be asked, and suggestions for replies.

When dinner was done that evening, he outlined the problem of the locks. "If there are combination locks . . ."

Phoebe Twinkle interrupted to ask what that term meant.

"The kinds that have numbers around in a circle and you turn the dial to your numbers to open them."

"Does everybody have to have a different combination that the porter has to remember?" Phoebe asked.

"I suppose so. That's the problem in a nutshell. There will be at least two or three hundred boxes. That's about how many people still live in Voorburg, I'd guess," Robert said.

"I don't think there are that many," Lily said. "Haven't you noticed how many businesses and houses have been abandoned by people going to California?"

"Okay, I'll check on this, but it's not really the problem I'm currently worried about."

Phoebe, who had raised the question of combinations, suddenly stood up and came as close to shouting as a lady could. "I've had a Eureka idea. Give the three snoops one combination for all three of their boxes, then give everyone one of two combinations."

"How will that help?" Robert asked.

Lily said, "Robert, you're being uncharacteristically dim-witted. The three old ladies will soon discover that their combinations are the same as one another's and assume, incorrectly, that everybody else's are the same. While in fact, half of them are another combination and the other half are a third combination. The porter can certainly remember all three."

Phoebe chimed in again. "Have the old ladies' boxes in the middle, set up vertically. And one combination for the boxes to the right of them and immediately above them—the other combination below them and to the left."

Everybody at the table except Robert was happy with

the solution. But he was a little sorry that two young women figured out what he couldn't. Harry Harbinger hadn't thought this out, nor had the stationmaster, except to ask questions about the locks.

All three of them failed to come up with a possible solution. And the women had had several suggestions. This was a concept that scared Robert.

CHAPTER THREE

Wednesday, April 19

ROBERT HAD THE SENSE that this postal project wasn't going to be as easy as he'd originally imagined. He needed to know the approximate number of people who currently lived in Voorburg-on-Hudson and outlying areas that were still being farmed. How could he find this out?

Where would Edwin McBride sort the mail? Not on the middle of the floor of the train station. That would create an equally chaotic situation as there was now.

Then there were the combination locks to think of. Even if McBride had a table near the boxes, he'd have to have all the doors open at the same time to sort them into the right boxes.

And what would happen to big packages, like the one he'd had shipped to himself with Lily's birthday present?

The post office boxes couldn't be that big or they'd take up all the walls of the station.

Who would know the answers to this multitude of queries?

He'd have to go back first to Harry Harbinger. After all, Harry and his brother had to make the sorting area and allow for the hardware.

When he caught up with Harry Wednesday morning, Robert was surprised that the town's best handyman had already given Robert's ideas some thought.

"I don't like the idea of combination locks built into the doors. For one thing, it's expensive. And nobody knows yet what this is going to cost."

"What's an alternative?" Robert asked.

"Well, there are keys, of course. But people would lose them and the lock would need to be changed on a lot of them from time to time. My brother and I won't agree to be responsible for this."

"Is there another alternative?" Robert whined.

"Oh, sure. Hardware that could take a combination lock. A piece of metal with a hole in it sticking out on the door, and another on the strip that separates the boxes. The person renting the box would supply for himself or herself a combination lock to slip through both holes. Some people know they don't get things that the snoops would be interested in, so they wouldn't even have to buy a combination lock."

"Brilliant!" Robert exclaimed. "Now, how and where will Mr. McBride sort the mail?"

Harry rolled his eyes at this question. "Robert, think about this. The inside of that station is *huge*. It was built around the turn of the century when Voorburg had a much bigger population. There was even a hotel my dad told us about, for wives and children. The husbands came on the weekends."

Robert said, "So?"

Patiently Harry explained. "There is plenty of space to set the box thing out into the room with a sorting room behind it. I've measured how much scrap wood I have, and I can make two hundred boxes that are four inches wide, four inches high, and nine inches deep. They'll be open at the back, and I'll build a long skinny table that can be used to sort the mail by box number. Same as the number on the front of the box."

This time Robert actually slapped his head. "I guess there's a door to this back room?"

Harry was getting frustrated. "Did you think Mr. McBride could crawl in through a letter box?"

"But, Harry, we don't know how many people there are in Voorburg. Will two hundred boxes be enough?"

"They'll *have* to be enough. When they're done, McBride can sell lottery tickets for them. Twenty-five cents each ticket. That will help fund his payment, and if the town council coughs up the initial cost, McBride could pay back a dime for each ticket. And I assume you're expecting people who have the winning numbers to also pay some small amount a year to use them. That's how you could reimburse the costs—if the town council agrees to funding the plan. Half to McBride, half until the city is paid back."

"Of course," Robert said as if he'd already thought of this. He hadn't. And suspected Harry knew it.

"You don't happen to know what became of my can of red paint, do you?" Harry asked.

"I didn't even know you had one," Robert replied.

"Mrs. White wanted a little chest painted red for her adopted girls. I had it almost finished and my paint and best brush disappeared."

Robert said, "I'll keep an eye out for anyone painting something red. Thanks for your advice about the mail."

Later on Monday, Robert learned how the stolen can of paint had been used. He'd decided to drop in at Mr. Kurtz's new shop to find out how business was going so far. He was shocked when he saw Mr. Kurtz and his granddaughter scraping a red swastika off the front window of the tailor shop with razor blades. "Wait!" Robert exclaimed. "Have you called the chief of police about this? He needs to know. Look here," he pointed at a faint blob of extra paint. "It's a fingerprint. Don't scrape it off until Chief Walker sees it."

Mr. Kurtz objected. His face was pale and frantic. "How could someone think I was a Nazi? I came halfway around the world to escape them."

"You need to sit down inside and wait until I call Chief Walker."

"Grandpa, Mr. Brewster is right."

"I don't want anyone else seeing this," he said firmly, going back to scraping.

"Then leave that fingerprint where it is," Robert said, pointing it out to Mr. Kurtz again.

Chief Walker arrived in ten minutes. "I don't know how to remove a painted fingerprint and keep it intact. I'm going to have to call in an expert to lift it where it is."

He went inside to call for help while Mr. Kurtz kept scraping at the swastika. His granddaughter came inside and so did Robert.

"Sit down and keep an eye on your grandfather so he doesn't scrape off the fingerprint and I'll make us some coffee," Robert said, wondering how much coffee he'd need, having never made it himself. "Or maybe we should do it the other way?" he asked Mrs. Smithson.

"You don't know how to make coffee, right?" Mrs. Smithson said with a knowing smile.

"Unfortunately not. Has your grandfather had customers yet?"

"Yes. Mrs. White came in with some of her little girls' dresses to have the hems let down. She said she'd taken one of her dresses that needed taking in to the tailor in Cold Spring, and he was rude. Not only that, he did a very bad job. She was sure my grandfather would do a better job. She's such a nice woman, and I've never heard her complain. But she was bitter about the other tailor. She'd bought a dress that was on sale without trying it on, and the seam at the shoulder was wrong. Too wide. That tailor just pinned it, and even poked her arm with a pin. When she went back, he'd just folded the fabric back into the shoulder and made the sleeves bunch up. Grandpa told her to bring the dress in when she picked up the little girls' dresses and he'd fix it correctly."

Mrs. Smithson went on, supposing Robert was more interested than he really was. "She brought in those adorable little girls she adopted to have their dresses let out at the hems. They're getting taller. Grandpa told her the dresses wouldn't look good that way. The inside color wouldn't match the outside. So he took her back where he has all his fabrics and let her choose fabrics that matched some of the colors in the dresses and added them to the bottom hems, sort of like petticoats. He also told the girls how pretty they were."

"Mrs. White is dotty about those little girls," Robert said. "Anybody else come in?"

"Later on a man came in and just looked around."

"Did you recognize him?"

"Never saw him before."

"What did he look like?"

"I didn't pay much attention. I was fixing Grandpa a sandwich. A smallish man, shorter than I. Not quite clean, skinny. Thinning brown hair. Grandpa asked if he needed anything tailored. The man just shrugged. He was watching as Grandpa was hanging up his shears on the back wall, and putting his other things in drawers under the counter. I'll make the coffee. Keep a close eye on Grandpa."

Watching Mr. Kurtz wasn't as easy as it sounded. The old man had almost finished scraping off the swastika and was eyeing the extra blob of paint. As he approached it, Robert said, "You can't scrape that off until the fingerprint man gets here."

"Yes, I will. My window must be clean."

Robert had to cup his hand carefully over the paint spot to keep the tailor from destroying it. Kurtz was angry, and he went inside to get a damp rag to clean up the paint that had fallen onto the sill of the window. Robert maintained his uncomfortable stance, until Chief Walker and the fingerprint expert arrived half an hour later. By then

Robert's right shoulder and wrist were in agony from holding his hand cupped over the fingerprint.

"I've never seen such a fingerprint," the expert said with a laugh. "Talk about a stupid crook." He rummaged through the bag he'd brought along, dusted some powder over the fingerprint, lifted it with a bit of sticky paper, and put the paper in a small box with great care. "It will take a while to compare this to our list of known criminals."

"How long?" Robert asked.

"Probably a week. Maybe more."

"May Mr. Kurtz scrape it off? He's determined to do so."

"I probably should take a second sample then," the fingerprint expert said. "Just to be sure we have a good copy, and so someone else can help me search the records we have on file."

"Do it now, please," Robert begged. "My arm aches from protecting it."

When the two boxes had been taken away, Mr. Kurtz immediately scraped away the fingerprint. Then he proceeded to clean the entire window with rags and vinegar.

Chief Walker asked if Robert had already had breakfast. Robert admitted he had, but said, "I could do with another. Mrs. Prinney has run out of flour so there was no bread this morning. First time it's ever happened."

Howard complained, "The woman at the boardinghouse tried to use last night's corned beef in a horrible omelet. The corned beef had dried out and the eggs were overcooked. Let's go to Mabel's and have a good early lunch. There's something I want to talk to you about."

They were both so hungry that they didn't speak until they'd eaten. They were at a table at the very back of the restaurant and the place was almost deserted.

"Here's my question," Howard said, seeming somewhat reluctant to put it bluntly. "You take boarders at Grace and Favor. Miss Twinkle and Mrs. Tarkington. Would I qualify as another boarder?"

"Of course you would, I assume. The women, in particular, would like to have another man around, especially an officer of the law. But are you sure you want to be that far from town?"

"It's downhill all the way," Walker said, folding his napkin and putting it beside his empty plate. "Not as time consuming as fighting my way up the hill."

"But you'd need your telephone line run clear up there," Robert said. "I'm sure the household wouldn't want to be answering your calls."

"I've thought about that and priced it. What I'd save on the boardinghouse room and the tiny overflow office there would more than make up for the cost of a telephone line. I'm sick to death of my clothes and hair smelling of cabbage. It's the pervasive odor of the entire boardinghouse I live in now."

"It takes a unanimous vote to accept a boarder," Robert told Howard. "But I'm sure it would be in your case."

Robert went on to explain what Mrs. Smithson had told him about Mrs. White's earlier visit to Mr. Kurtz and how downright angry she'd been at the other tailor.

"That's unusual. I've never heard her be critical of anyone. Robert, I hope you convince the people at Grace and Favor to save me from the cabbage stink."

That evening Robert was right. The same questions he'd asked Howard were asked of the residents and boarders and the maid Mimi.

He waited until after dinner to raise the issue of Howard's moving into Grace and Favor, and had asked Mrs. Prinney and Mimi to delay cleaning up after dinner for a few minutes.

All the women instantly agreed, as he had expected they would. For one thing, Howard Walker was good-looking, socially acceptable, and would increase their sense of safety, not that this was terribly important often.

It was Mr. Prinney, who raised the questions. "How would he take telephone calls? There's only one extra line, and that's in my home office."

Robert explained what Howard had said about having his own telephone line.

"And would he take all his meals here?" Mr. Prinney asked.

"Probably not," Robert said. "But we don't all eat every meal here. Mrs. Tarkington takes a packed lunch during the school year, and Phoebe always takes one to work at her hat shop. Chief Walker would probably eat lunch at Mabel's. It's closer to the jail in town, where he spends most of his time."

The only other decision involved was which room would suit him, and it was decided that it would probably be the one across the hallway from Mrs. Tarkington's. There was a connected bath on one side, and a closet on the other side of that room. And nobody would be bothered by a phone ringing on the second floor from a room next door.

The cost of the room would be decided by Mr. Prinney, in private consultation with Lily and Robert when they found out about Howard's luncheon plans.

Robert was pleased. Aside from Mr. Prinney, he was the only man who lived at Grace and Favor. And as much as he respected and liked Mr. Prinney, they were from different generations and didn't have a lot in common. The estate decisions that needed to be made rested mostly with Lily, who understood them far better than Robert did. It would be swell to have another man near his own age living with them.

CHAPTER FOUR

Thursday, April 20

THE NEXT MORNING, Robert went to the chief of police's office in town and told Howard he'd been unanimously approved to live at Grace and Favor.

"That's swell," Walker said. "I have to admit that I've already packed most of my clothes," he said with a grin.

"Come up first and see the room we've assigned you and make sure you like it."

They took both their cars, and Robert led Howard up the stairs and opened the door to the room the residents had decided might suit their newest boarder. As Howard walked in he said, "There's lots of light from those windows and it's a bigger room than the two rooms I had at the boardinghouse."

"Sorry it's not a river view," Robert said.

"I've lived right by the river and don't need to see it again. It stinks even more than the boardinghouse."

"Here's the bathroom," Robert said, opening a door.

Howard looked more closely and said, "My *own* bathroom? I don't have to share it?" He grinned at Robert. "Worth the price and more. I've been sharing a bathroom with three other men for too long. What's more, one of them must have read a whole magazine every time he was in there. Speaking of price, what's it going to cost me?"

Robert gave him the price Mrs. Tarkington paid less two dollars. "She has the same sort of space, and a private bath. She gets breakfast, a packed lunch, and dinner. We're charging you a little less than we charge Mrs. Tarkington. She has a river view and likes it and is willing to pay for it."

"It's only two dollars more than what I'm paying now and well worth it. Do I have to pack my own lunch though? I like eating at Mabel's. It's closer to my office."

"No, Mrs. Prinney packs the lunches. But if you prefer to stay in town at lunchtime, we can take another dollar off. Oh, I haven't shown you the closet yet." Robert opened the double doors. The closet was enormous and flanked the main room on the other side.

"That's impressive," Howard said. "Almost as big as the second room at the boardinghouse where my office is. By the way, I've talked to the telephone people. They can run a line up here just like Mr. Prinney has for his office in town. And I can have two phones. One in this room and one in the front hall."

"Good idea. If we were all at dinner, you probably wouldn't hear it if it was ringing in your room. Ready to move in?"

"I won't be ready until the phone upstairs and in the hall is installed. The guy said he could do it tomorrow. Will you or Lily be around to show him where they go?"

"We'll both be here. And everybody is looking forward to having you live here."

"So am I," Howard said, shaking Robert's hand.

On Friday, Robert was a bit overeager to get Howard situated. Once the phone was scheduled to be installed the next morning, Robert insisted on helping Howard to haul most of his belongings at the boardinghouse to Grace and Favor. He insisted that the Duesie was much bigger than the chief's police car and they could get everything moved in one trip rather than three.

"You're being very kind, but I don't really need all this help."

"But I'm here and willing to cart boxes," Robert said.

They piled three large boxes into the big automobile that was the love of Robert's life, and headed up the hill.

Robert helped carry the boxes. Finally, everything was in Howard's new room.

Howard said, "Robert, you've been really helpful, but I'm not going to let you unpack for me. I'm going to take my time to figure out what should go where—and it would drive you mad the way I'm probably going to dither about for several days. Besides that, tomorrow I have to take away those files from the last case to be stored safely."

Howard wandered to the big window in the main room again, and happened to look down. "What's wrong with those shrubs?" he asked.

Robert joined him and looked where Walker was pointing. "They look as if they're diseased, don't they? Before the Harbinger boys start building the post office–style boxes, maybe they'd dig them up. If they have a disease it could spread to all the shrubs. The place would look naked without greenery around the first floor. Okay, I'm leaving you to it. I won't interfere anymore."

"It might be bagworms," Howard said. "Those are—"

Robert put his hands over his ears. "Oh, please don't describe them to me. The name alone makes me dizzy."

"Robert, you're such a sissy," Walker said with a laugh. "Now just go away, please."

Saturday morning, Lester Johnson, the man from the telephone exchange, arrived early. Robert was still dawdling over breakfast. As little as he wanted to hear about nature, let alone something called bagworms, he liked seeing how other people did their jobs. Not that he intended to learn how to replace them. He simply found it interesting to watch. He was showing Lester Johnson to Howard's room, and made a suggestion about where the phone ought to go. The man didn't appear to care about Robert's opinion.

"Leave it to me. I need to do some measurements between this room and the front hall. They appear to be pretty close to vertical. You know, when I had to go upstairs in Chief Walker's boardinghouse to install his phone, I nearly gagged at the smell. I'm sure he'll be happier here."

Robert walked down the stairs behind Johnson. More measuring. More figuring with a blunt pencil in a shabby notebook. "Yes, it's going to work out fine. I don't need anymore help, sir."

Robert was miffed. He wanted to follow him around and see what he did. But he was clearly unwelcome to do so.

An hour later, Lester Johnson hunted down Robert and said, "Want to watch?"

"Sure, I do."

"You go upstairs and see if the phone there works. I'll stay here to see if it rings here."

Robert hot-footed it upstairs, just in time to hear the second ring. "Hi, Letty," Robert said to the girl at the exchange. "Connect me to the chief of police, if he's back from his errand, then hang up." When he connected, he heard the click as Letty pulled out her plug.

"Hi, Howard. It's Robert. I'm on your upstairs telephone. And Lester Johnson is presumably on the one in the downstairs hall."

There was a snort from the repairman. "Chief, both of them work. You want the other one at the boardinghouse disabled today?"

There was another click and the repairman said, "Letty, we all heard that. This is Lester Johnson. You and I both work for the same outfit, see? If you do this to me again, I'll report you to him."

"Yes, si—" The click off was so fast she missed the last letter of the word.

Howard and Robert were both laughing. Howard said, "Lester, you're a braver man than I am."

"You want the boardinghouse line shut down now, Chief?"

"If you would. I'm pleased this worked," he said.

"Drop by the jail when you're finished so I can pay you for your work. Good-bye, Robert."

Chief Walker walked over to the boardinghouse. He said to the woman who owned it, "I'm just picking up the last of my belongings. The telephone gentleman will be here in a few minutes to cut off my connection. He'll do it from outside the building and won't bother you."

"Good for you," she said with bitter sarcasm. "What do you think I'm going to do with these two rooms you've been renting? With a door between them? Nobody else will be able to afford two rooms."

"Then put a lock on the door," Howard said bluntly. "I only have one more drawer to empty. Good luck, miss."

He grinned all the way upstairs, removed his shaving materials, a hairbrush and comb, and put everything in a paper bag.

There was no sign of the owner or any of the other boarders when he came back down. He went back to his small office at the jail to wait for Lester Johnson. When he'd thanked him again and paid him, he headed up the hill to Grace and Favor.

Robert was in the kitchen, chatting with Mrs. Prinney about how nice it was going to be to have Howard living at Grace and Favor. Howard came in and asked Mrs.

Prinney if he could hang his uniform and some of his other clothes on the drying line outside.

"Yes, that's perfectly all right. But why?"

"To get the smell of cabbage and cheap sausage out of them. Then I'm taking a shower later to get the smell out of my hair," he said with a grin.

"You don't like cabbage and sausage?" Mrs. Prinney asked. "I'll remember that."

"No, I've eaten yours here before and it's much better and doesn't stink up the whole house. I didn't mean to insult your cooking. You're the best cook I've ever known, including my own grandmother."

Saturday night, dinner was a gala event. Everyone dressed up as a welcome to their new boarder. Howard wore his best suit, which had been hung outside and pressed and brushed up by Mimi. Phoebe and Mrs. Tarkington wore their best dresses and little hats that looked almost like tiaras.

Mrs. Prinney had shed her apron and had stuffed herself into her tightest corset. Robert wore his old tux. It wasn't as nice as before, but in dim light it looked fairly good. Especially since it had a blinding white starched collar that almost glowed. He wore the gold watch his father had given him when he graduated from the private high school he'd attended.

Even Lily, who almost never wore jewelry, wore her late mother's diamond and sapphire earrings and the matching ring. She'd given away most of her best frocks because she'd lost so much weight during the two years of horror after the stock market crashed. Two whole years in a dirty tenement apartment on the fifth floor of a cold-water flat in New York City. But she'd kept three of her favorite dresses and had taken one—a light coral–colored floor-length silk—to the new tailor in town. In a matter of two hours he'd fixed it so it fit perfectly.

Mrs. Prinney's best china graced the table along with her solid silver place settings. The napkins were pure white linen. Candles glowed and there were cut-glass wineglasses to serve two fine old dusty bottles Robert had found in the wine cellar. Unfortunately, the smaller bottle had gone a bit off, but the diners finished off the large bottle. The meal was roasted pork with a very good gravy, two salads, fresh young peas, and scalloped potatoes.

After a floating island—dessert—they all stood and toasted the new boarder.

"This isn't an every night sort of meal, is it?" Howard asked.

He stood up, holding his glass, and toasted everyone else. "The nicest people I know all at the same table. I'm the luckiest man alive."

Robert glanced at Lily, who was threatening to tear up again. In fact, Robert himself was close to doing so as well. It had been a wonderful evening.

CHAPTER FIVE

Monday, April 24

AS A NEW WEEK STARTED, nobody but Lily and Robert were at Grace and Favor. The Harbinger boys were supposed to cut out the diseased bushes, but had to beg off until later in the day because Miss Twibell at the nursing home nearby wanted the dumbwaiter rails regreased. They were catching near the basement. The dumbwaiter had been Robert's idea and he was proud of it, and he didn't even want to look at the nasty bushes anyway.

Mr. Prinney was at his office in the village; Phoebe Twinkle was at her hat shop; Mrs. Prinney was supervising a two-day bake sale to raise money for a family in town who needed some help because the father of three children had run off to California. Chief Walker was working at his office at the jail. Mimi, who'd done an early morning blitz of cleaning, was visiting her dreadful aunts for the day.

Even Lily was absent in a sense. Her dog Agatha had gone outside early in the day and rolled in a very dead animal and came back stinking to high heaven. Lily was bathing her.

Robert went to the library with his lock picks and the somewhat blurry and badly spelled instructions. The library had a long sideboard on the left side of the room with locked bookshelves above. Nobody had ever been able to find a key to open them. So Robert started at the far left end. With a little practice, he managed to get one of the doors open. He took out a book titled *The Biography of Leonard Spokes.* It was the first one on the left of the bottom shelf.

It looked hefty, but was surprisingly lightweight. He opened the book and stared with astonishment. It wasn't a real book. It was a box filled with ten-dollar bills.

"Holy Toledo!" he said.

He took out the next book, titled *The Persian Wars.* That one was filled with five-dollar bills.

He put both books back and gently closed the door without relocking it, and galloped up the stairs to Lily's room. He knocked on the bathroom door.

Lily called out, "Open the door, but you'll be sorry. Agatha found a long-dead animal in the woods and rolled in it."

The room stank and Lily had the window wide open and a little fan sitting on the sill blowing out the smell.

Agatha was wrapped in a towel, looking terribly pleased with herself for gaining all this interest.

"Lily, you must come down to the library to see what I discovered," Robert said, nearly yelling.

"What?"

"You must see it for yourself."

"Take Agatha down to the kitchen to dry off and let me take a shower first. I smell almost as bad as she did."

"Believe me, this can't wait. Someone might come home before you see what I found."

"At least let me change my clothes and pin a scarf around my stinking hair."

With Agatha settled on a rug in front of the oven, he headed back to the library just as Lily descended the stairs. She followed him into the library. "So?" she asked.

With a flourish, Robert opened the library door that concealed the books.

"Good heavens! You found a key?"

"Not exactly," Robert said. "Take out that book"—he pointed at it and went on—"titled *The Biography of Leonard Stokes* and open it."

Lily did so and almost yelped. "Money! Have you counted it?"

"Not yet. Now open *The Persian Wars.*"

"Five-dollar bills. Robert, do you suppose that *all* of these books are fake and full of cash?"

"One can only hope," Robert said, grinning like a madman.

"We must tell Mr. Prinney about this. I wonder if he might have known all along. Maybe he has the key, come to think of it." She paused and said, "What did you mean when you said 'not exactly'?"

Robert confessed. "I took a day off to go to New York—"

"I remember that."

"I bought a set of lock picks from a bum in Central Park."

"Lock picks! Aren't they illegal?"

"I didn't inquire," Robert said.

"We must tell Mr. Prinney about this."

"Why?"

"Oh, Robert. Don't be silly. These fake books are part of Great-uncle Horatio's estate. Mr. Prinney is the executor. He must be informed."

Grudgingly, Robert admitted that she was right. "But do I have to admit to the lock picks?"

"How else could you explain opening the door to the shelves?"

They were interrupted by an extremely loud grinding noise from the front of the house. Lily yelped, "Put the books back, close the door, and hide the lock picks. Whatever is that racket?"

Robert did as she asked and inadvertently closed the door to the shelves. Lily wasn't there to hear the expletive he voiced. *Oh, well,* he thought, *I got it open once. I can do it again.* He followed Lily and discovered that it was the Harbinger boys. They were almost concealed behind the bushes in front of the mansion.

"*Yo!*" Robert bellowed. The noise stopped and Harry came around carrying the scariest saw Robert had ever seen.

"What is that thing?" Robert shouted.

Harry turned off the machine. "What did you say?"

"I asked what that is," Robert said.

"It's my new Stihl gas-powered chain saw. This is the first time I've used it. Cuts through like a hot knife through butter," Harry said proudly.

Harry's younger brother, Jim, came struggling through the prickly bush that remained. "Isn't that the bee's knees?" he asked.

Robert considered telling the truth—that this was the most frightening gadget he'd ever seen.

Harry was twenty-nine and two years older than his brother Jim, as well as being taller, sturdier, and smarter. Their father had been a general contractor and taught them how to roof, paint, make furniture, and a variety of other skills. But their dad warned them about doing electrical things. "Electricians get killed more often than any other trade," he said. "Still, rich or poor, there are always people needing repairs they don't know how to do."

"So were the bushes diseased?" Lily asked, looking at the stumps. She hadn't joined the men until the noise had stopped.

"No. But look up," Harry said.

Both Lily and Robert did as he said. "There's a roof up at the top that overhangs the house," Lily said. "Is that what you're pointing out?"

"Yes," Harry said. "They were dying of drought."

"But the bushes look ancient. How did they suddenly die of drought?"

"Miss Brewster," Harry said very politely, "haven't you noticed how little rain we've had the last couple years?"

"We never knew. We haven't been here for decades like some people in Voorburg," Robert said. Thinking this might have sounded surly, he amended, "I wish we had."

"Why did you cut off all the branches and leave the trunks?" Lily asked.

"Because we're going to take the trunks out by themselves," Harry said. "Hook them up to the truck with ropes and pull them out. We'll bring some gravel in for drainage when it starts to rain again. If you want new shrubs here, plant them farther away from the foundation so they get more water."

"Good advice," Lily said.

"What's that smell?" Jim said, looking at Lily as he stood beside her.

"Me," Lily said. "Or rather my dog. She rolled in some dead creature and I just bathed her, but I haven't washed the stench off myself yet."

Harry said, "Jim, quit embarrassing Miss Brewster and help me with digging out around these stumps, tying a chain around them so we can haul them to the dump."

Lily and Robert stood back to watch as the first stump was jerked out of the ground.

"Oh, how horrible!" she exclaimed as the big root ball was dragged a few feet away. "That's the skeleton of someone's hand sticking out of the roots." She sat down on the ground, breathing hard to keep from fainting.

Chief Walker was there in fifteen minutes. He'd looked at the hand and told the Harbinger boys to find a tarp to cover the hole. "Nobody touch anything. I'm going to call for some experts."

Chief Walker was lucky. He found two experts that were attending a professional meeting in Fishkill. There was a pathologist from Albany and an anthropologist from New York City with a bag of tools he'd been using to demonstrate techniques of detailed, careful investigation.

On Tuesday they were both at Grace and Favor. The pathologist, a Dr. Meredith, was all for simply digging up the rest of the bones as quickly as possible so he could examine them. The anthropologist disagreed. "Haste in such a case is wrong. He or she has been here a long time. There is no hurry and valuable hints might be lost."

He introduced himself as Dr. Sam Toller and set about getting out his equipment from a bag he'd brought along. He was a long-limbed, sandy-haired man in his late thirties. He had a perpetual smile.

The hole wasn't terribly deep and he and the Harbinger boys got flat on their stomachs with tiny trowels and small brushes he'd brought in the bag. "It's a good thing this is loose soil. It won't take long. All I need is the skull and pelvis to determine the age and sex of the victim."

Chief Walker was assigned to sit behind them with an assortment of paper bags in a variety of sizes. Robert went inside, fearing what nasty things might be revealed, but Lily stayed back, fascinated once she'd gotten over the shock. It was tedious work as the expert and the Harbingers kept delicately scooping away soil. Lily was assigned to sift the dirt in a set of sieves. First with large holes, then smaller ones, and then very fine ones. She was the first to notice the beads.

"Get someone to bring a big pot of warm water, would you, miss?" Dr. Toller said with excitement.

Dr. Meredith was impatient, but had found a bench not far away to sit and read a textbook he'd had in his automobile.

Robert was quick to return with a pot. The beads were swished gently and then the water was poured back out through the finest sieve. The beads turned out to be rather pretty balls about the size of a child's fingernail. They were various shades of brown, green, dark red, orange, and yellow, and had holes through them. "Whatever they were strung on at one time has been dissolved. They've been fired to make them this hard and durable," Dr. Toller said. "We'll keep sieving them."

The next discovery was a bit of leather about the size of a postage stamp. Toller said, "Probably deerskin that's been heavily oiled or beeswaxed. Otherwise it would have rotted."

"Are we talking about an Indian?" Chief Walker asked.

"Most likely. If it had been a white hunter, there probably wouldn't be the beads," Dr. Toller said. "We're progressing well. But I imagine everybody's hungry. At least I am."

"If Mrs. Prinney were here she'd make us lunch," Lily said.

"Let's just pack up and go to town to Mabel's," Chief Walker said.

Everybody went along, Chief Walker with the pathologist and the anthropologist in his police car. Robert, Lily, and the Harbinger boys in the Duesie. They discussed what had already been found with various levels of interest. Lily and Harry were the most enthusiastic about what they might learn about the skeleton. Jim was a bit bored with the chore of sifting and brushing around dirt when there were other things he and his brother needed to do for other customers.

Robert didn't want to see the rest of the bones. "Bones and bagworms all in one day," he said with a shudder. "It's too much to bear."

Lily said, "You've always been afraid of things in nature. Remember the day we first came here and you admitted that you were afraid of trees?"

"I never said that," Robert claimed.

"Yes, you did," Lily said, laughing and gently poking her elbow into his ribs.

Since Lily was right, he didn't pursue the conversation.

CHAPTER SIX

REFRESHED BY A HEARTY LUNCH, the anthropologist, Dr. Toller, was eager to unearth the rest of the skeleton. "I can see the front and top of the skull now and it's a young person," he said, addressing his remarks to Lily because she seemed the most interested. After delivering the pathologist and anthropologist, Chief Walker had left to investigate a house that had been broken into.

"How can you tell?" Lily asked Dr. Toller.

"By the way the various parts of skull come together. They don't entirely knit together until a person is close to eighteen or twenty. I'd guess the subject was perhaps early teens. Possibly as young as fifteen or even younger."

"You can't tell anything else from the skull?"

"Yes, the teeth indicate it's an American Indian."

"They have different teeth?"

"Yes, the front ones are 'shoveled.' That means that they—" He thought for a moment how to describe it to a stranger. "The calcium they're made of goes around the sides and they are a bit concave at the back. Sort of like a little shovel."

"That's fascinating. I'd have never guessed front teeth weren't always the same," Lily responded.

He nearly preened. It wasn't often that an attractive young woman found his information interesting. He'd never had a young woman sign up for his classes, and most of the young men who took the class did so because they thought it would be easy to get a good grade. He'd only had two young men, on average, each year, who seemed genuinely interested in the subject that fascinated him.

"What's more," he went on, knowing he was showing off, "the molars, as far as I can see before the skull is totally released from the soil where it is resting, aren't worn down at all."

"And what does that mean?"

"Most of the tribes in this part of the country ate a lot of corn, ground to powder between two stones. Some of the stone dust gets into it. It gradually files down the molars. But let's get back to work. I'll try to get the entire skull out. And Harry and Jim, you can get on with pulling the other stump out. But go easy, if you can. We don't want to destroy any evidence."

The Harbinger brothers soon eased the stump out of its hole with the chain and the truck. Dr. Toller looked over the bottom of the ball of roots and said, "There don't seem to be any bones attached to this one. But just put it aside. I want to look more carefully at it later."

He stared into the hole, obviously anxious to see what they'd find under the dirt. But he doggedly went back to unearthing the skull.

Harry thought this was interesting, but even he was becoming a bit annoyed at how long it was taking. He'd expected to be finished with this easy job in one morning and then get back to other higher-paying jobs. They had two people right now waiting for Harry and Jim—one with a sagging, dangerous porch, and another customer with a leaking roof.

When Emmaline Prinney arrived, flushed with victory, the bake sale having made a record amount of money, she was slightly alarmed by all the people in front of Grace and Favor, most of them looking at two holes. One of the two people she didn't recognize was on his stomach doing something in the hole.

As she watched, he pulled up a big ball of dirt, washed it off in a bucket, and brought out a dirty skull.

She joined the group and touched Lily's arm. "What in the world is going on here?"

"The Harbinger boys pulled up a stump of a bush yesterday, and there was a skeletal hand sticking out of the roots. Didn't anyone tell you?"

"No. I guess I was in the kitchen baking all day. Why didn't anyone mention it over dinner?"

"I don't know," Lily apologized. "I guess we were all just too hungry to mention it."

"I'll need to go back to town to get things to make late-afternoon sandwiches for this crowd," Mrs. Prinney said, not sounding the least put out. She always loved to feed a crowd.

Dr. Toller was happily examining the skull. "No damage. He or she wasn't struck on the head." Then he started carefully removing the rib cage and the upper part of the spine. Washing them off, setting them down in order on a paper bag. He said to Lily, "They have to dry before I can number them for bagging."

Lily was once again struck by how very cheerful he was about this. But the day was turning dark and a cold breeze had sprung up so she went inside for a while. Watching a rib cage dry wasn't really all that interesting.

Mrs. Prinney wasn't the only resident of Grace and Favor who had an obsession. Hers was cooking, but Mimi's great love was cleaning. Even as a child of seven, her late mother had cleaned for Mr. Horatio's aunt Flora and sometimes let Mimi come along. When Flora Brewster died, and left the house to Mr. Horatio, he kept Mimi and her mother on. After Horatio died, Mimi's mother had passed on, and the new Brewster brother and sister moved in. By then, she'd loved cleaning. She'd cover most of her curly platinum blond hair in a bright kerchief and she always wore an apron when she worked.

When Mrs. Prinney asked Mimi to tidy up the big room at the far end of the second floor for the pathologist and the anthropologist, she added, "Then take away their clothes and brush them out. They're both muddy and may not have brought along a change of attire."

Naturally Mimi didn't need to clean the rooms. She dusted and shook out the rugs almost every day anyway. And she couldn't clean their clothes until they changed what they were wearing.

Mrs. Prinney naturally provided the late-afternoon snack and invited the two strangers to join them for dinner and stay the night.

"Harry and Jim," she added, "you two are welcome to stay for dinner as well."

"Thank you, Mrs. Prinney, but Mom has planned a roast for dinner," Harry said.

"Thank you, too," his brother Jim whispered when they were alone for a few minutes. "I'm sick of this job and these scientific fellows."

"I think it's interesting. But I don't want to be roped into more work today. Nor tomorrow for that matter. We have other jobs we promised to do and they expect us to show up when we said we would."

After dinner, Robert quietly alerted Mr. Prinney and Lily that he wanted a private meeting with them. Mr. Prinney didn't ask why, but his curiosity was clear.

Mrs. Prinney and Mimi were tending to the two guests, both of whom had a change of clothes so Mimi could just brush up and press the things they'd worn all day; Chief Walker had gone to his office in town to clear up some paperwork; Mrs. Tarkington had retired early to read a book; and Phoebe was in her own room turning up a hem for one of her best customers. Mrs. Prinney was already preparing a dessert for the next day.

Lily and Robert could count on getting Mr. Prinney

to themselves, where in the library the threesome would not be disturbed.

But just in case, Robert suggested that Mr. Prinney lock the door from the inside for a short time.

"Why is that?" the attorney asked.

"You'll see in a moment," Robert said.

Robert had gone in earlier in the day, again picking the lock where the books he'd discovered yesterday—filled with money—were. He'd shut the glass door, but had done so carefully so that the lock didn't engage. He signaled to Mr. Prinney to come close and opened the door.

"You found a key?" Mr. Prinney exclaimed.

"Not exactly. I found another way to open it. I want you to look at two of these books. He selected the two that he and Lily had examined and put them on the big table in the middle of the room. "Open them, please."

"Good heavens! I—I hardly know what to say. I always believed these were all real books," Mr. Prinney said.

"Maybe the rest of them are," Lily said.

Mr. Prinney closed both books. "Did you count the money in these?"

"We didn't have time," Robert said.

Mr. Prinney moved to one of the comfortable chairs by the French doors to the balcony outside. He sat silently for a long time, and both siblings kept a good eye on him, wondering what he was thinking.

Finally Mr. Prinney tented his fingers and said, "I have to admit that I'm a bit disappointed."

"What is there to be disappointed about?"

"Your great-uncle didn't live here very long between his Aunt Flora's death and his own, but as soon as he moved to Voorburg, he put all his financial matters in my hands. Then later, he had me write his will. I thought I knew about all his assets, but he never mentioned the money in the fake books. I knew he'd sold all his stock early in 1929. That was when he bought the then-fertile farms in the Midwest, and the extensive properties near Los Angeles. Later he mentioned that he should have waited until later because the stock market hit its all-time high a month or two before the Crash. I suspect now that he did hold on to some of it until then and took the money in cash."

Lily said, "It would naturally make you sad to know that, if that's the case, he didn't confide in you at the time."

"Well, now it's neither here nor there," Mr. Prinney said rather prissily. "What we need to do is take a tally of what's here." He paused for a moment and frowned. "Robert, a few minutes ago you told me you hadn't found the key. How did you manage to open the glass door?"

Robert had the good grace to look embarrassed. "That day I went to New York, remember?"

"Yes, I made a note of it, per your great-uncle's will."

"I was shopping for Lily's birthday and met up with a guy on a street next to Central Park who sold me a set of lock picks and a badly written set of instructions."

"You *picked* the lock?"

"Yes," Robert admitted. "Everyone who lives here has commented at one time or another wondering why the bookcases are locked, and there is no sign of a key."

"What do we do now?" Lily asked. "Is it our money? It apparently isn't mentioned in the will. Does that mean we can't use it until we serve our full ten years of providing for ourselves?"

"It's a tricky question, isn't it?" Mr. Prinney agreed. "The intention of his will is that you have to earn your own living for ten years. However, whatever money is here wasn't accounted for. I'll have to think this out carefully. But first, we need a complete account of how much cash is here."

"How are we going to explain this to the rest of the residents? We need to lock them out," Lily said in her usual practical manner.

Robert said, "Couldn't we just say that the library is out of bounds until some important estate business is completed?"

"We could," Lily said, "but this seems to be everybody's favorite room in which to sit and smoke, read, play cards, listen to the radio, or have a drink. Besides, Mimi would go haywire if she couldn't dust and polish in here every day."

"How's this?" Robert suggested. "We let Mimi come in to clean first thing in the morning, then we lock it up for a couple of hours a day. Lily makes a detailed account of how much was in every book. After she's done, we put the books back. Then Mr. Prinney locks the records up in the safe at his office. We just keep adding to the records."

Lily gawked. "Robert, that's brilliant. I applaud you for this idea. Frankly, I wouldn't want to spend whole days counting money. Much as I like cash."

CHAPTER SEVEN

DR. MEREDITH, the pathologist, had packed up and left early that Wednesday morning, saying to Lily as he saw her come down the stairs, "Dr. Toller isn't going to release that skeleton until he's through with it." He clearly disapproved of this behavior. "I could see him last night from my bedroom window. He was crouched over the hole where the second bush was with a lantern, digging around. I do appreciate your letting me stay overnight, and have thanked Mrs. Prinney for putting me up and feeding me, and left a tip for the maid. I wish I had time to stay and thank everyone."

"No thanks are required, Dr. Meredith. Mrs. Prinney loves to cook, and the maid loves to clean. It was nice to meet you. Have a good trip home."

As the residents assembled for breakfast, Mr. Prinney

announced that the library would be closed and locked for several days from eight in the morning until eleven. It would be open for Mimi to clean or anyone to visit until one in the afternoon. It would be locked again at that time and be free to use by four-thirty. He emphasized that he, Robert, and Lily had important information to go over regarding the estate. It wouldn't interest or influence anyone else who lived at Grace and Favor.

Everyone was naturally curious. Emmaline Prinney took her husband aside in his home office and asked, "The estate isn't in financial trouble, is it?"

"Don't worry. Quite the opposite is true. But I can't tell you more," he assured her.

When Chief Walker, Mrs. Tarkington, and Phoebe Twinkle left for work, Mr. Prinney joined Robert and Lily in the library, saying, "Robert, get your lock picks and open this first door again. Lily, would you use the fresh ledger I put on the big table to take down what Robert and I count and name the book the cash came from?"

"I'd be glad to be the one sitting down comfortably," Lily said with a sigh. "My back hurts a bit from bending down yesterday to wash off all those beads."

Robert already had the hang of the lock picks, and they got started.

After the third book in the row, which contained well-used one-dollar bills, Elgin Prinney took down the fourth one, and it was half full of fifty-dollar bills. There was, to his surprise, a sheet of paper in Horatio Brewster's handwriting on top of the fake book.

"Hmm," Mr. Prinney said. "It was as I suspected. He did leave money in the market until it reached its last peak and demanded cash for what remained. But there's more."

He handed the sheet of paper to Robert to read the rest. "It reads as this," Robert said. " 'If either of my heirs are canny or ambitious enough to open this case before the duration of the specific terms of my will, regarding the ten years, they will be allowed to open one book at six-month intervals and share equally and with Mr. Prinney, Esquire, the proceeds. I threw the key in the river. Not all the books in this bank of shelves contain anything, and my heirs aren't allowed to open another one when that is the case. All the other bookcases are all real books. If they wish to read them, they may do so. At the end of the ten years, if they've followed the conditions of the will, the rest will be theirs at that time.'

" 'Signed this last day of September, 1929, by Horatio Brewster.' "

"Does this mean we get the tens in the first book now?" Lily asked.

"I suppose so," Mr. Prinney replied.

Robert retrieved the first book, and he and Mr. Prinney counted out the ten-dollar bills. "A nice round nine hundred dollars. Three hundred for Lily, me, and you, Mr. Prinney."

"I don't think I can accept my share," Mr. Prinney said. "After all, I live in a great big house that isn't mine for free."

"But that's what Great-uncle Horatio wanted," Lily said. "What's more, you do your share by taking care of the estate for us. You should be paid for it."

"Lily's right," Robert agreed. "You must take your share. Sometimes, according to this letter, it won't be anything."

"I'm giving a quarter of mine to a charity," Lily said. "Maybe the Red Cross or something else that's providing help for the poor."

"I'll do the same," Robert said, not quite as enthusiastically as Lily.

"So shall I then," Mr. Prinney said.

"Will you keep our shares in the safe here?" Lily asked. "I want to think who to give it to first. And I don't want to hide it under my mattress."

"I'd be glad to. I don't suppose we need to take account of all these books right now. We already know what's in the first ones we opened."

"Couldn't we at least shake the rest of them and see if they're real books, or just empty boxes?" Robert asked.

"I don't think we're supposed to do that," Mr. Prinney

said. "The letter from your great-uncle doesn't specifically mention such a thing."

"I thought you'd say that," Robert said with a hint of self-pity.

"Let's divvy up the money and Mr. Prinney can put it in the safe," Lily said. "I want to see what else Dr. Toller has found under the other bush."

"You're letting yourself in for a lot more work helping him," Robert warned.

"I know. But I find this skeleton business interesting. I might spend some of my money taking some classes about anthropology."

"God forgive. You can't mean that you're going to be dragging bones in here for your homework, can you?"

"I just might," Lily said, handing her share of the tens to Mr. Prinney.

To prove it, Lily went outside to see what Dr. Toller was doing today. The second bush had been turned over and apparently inspected for anything interesting.

"Anything in the roots of the bush, sir?" she asked.

"Not a thing," Dr. Toller said. "I'm up to the pelvis of the body but can't go on until I've dug down to the legs and feet. Would you like to help?"

"I'm a little afraid of digging into something I shouldn't. But I'll sift and dispose of dirt you take out if you'd like."

"That would indeed be a help. I was hoping those two nice young Harbinger boys would be back today to help out again."

"Harry probably will be here eventually but Jim isn't especially interested, I'm sorry to say. Harry found this as fascinating as I do," Lily said, not at all sure this was the complete truth. Harry was the smarter of the two and if decisions about a roof were required, he was the one who needed to be there to decide how it was to be done properly.

Dr. Toller had accumulated a lot of buckets to wash off the bones and others to put the dirt in. Then the dirt would be returned to the holes in the ground after the sifting. Each time he excavated a bucket full of soil, he'd pass it up to her to put on the pile that was rapidly building up.

Pretty soon she could see the skeleton's upper legs start to appear, then the knees. "Does this tell you anything?"

"Just that she did a lot of things squatting. Probably grinding corn on a stone, or making the balls of clay that the beads were made of. Young as she is, there seem to be slight signs of rickets as well."

"What are rickets?" Lily asked.

"It's a little complicated. You need calcium to grow good bones, but it's impossible to do so without vitamin D."

"How do you get vitamin D?"

"From sunshine mostly," Dr. Toller said. "She may have grown up in a cave."

"Wouldn't there have been a fire in the cave?" Lily asked.

"Probably. But a wood fire doesn't provide enough natural light, or none at all, I suppose."

As he was still uncovering the legs of the skeleton Lily made up an excuse to go help Mrs. Prinney with something she was preparing for dinner.

An hour later, Dr. Toller came in and asked Mimi where Miss Brewster was. "I have something important to show her."

Mimi delivered the message to Lily, who was in her bedroom, reading a book with Agatha lying at the bottom of her bed.

She ran downstairs, Agatha so excited that something interesting might be happening that she was right on Lily's heels.

Dr. Toller was deep in the hole. "Look at her feet."

Lily squatted down to look. The skeleton was wearing pretty moccasins, entirely intact. Dr. Toller had carefully removed them and washed them off. They had tiny, pretty beads all over the front.

"How on earth did those survive?" she asked.

"Beeswax, most likely. I can't think of anything else

that would have so thoroughly impregnated the leather well enough to preserve them so perfectly. I also have unearthed the pelvis."

"What are you going to do with the skeleton now that you have the whole thing?"

"I owe it to the pathologist to send it to him. We've agreed that once he's gone over it, it will go into a museum. Someday, someone will figure out how to date old bones. I hope it's within my lifetime. Do you think the Harbinger boys would make me a crate in which to ship her?"

"Why are you calling the skeleton 'her'?" Lily asked.

Only slightly embarrassed to explain in detail, he merely said, "A woman's pelvis is designed to separate to let a baby's head through the birth canal. A man's isn't."

Her, Lily thought. She'd still been thinking of the skeleton as "it." From now on, the skeleton would be a girl.

Dr. Toller was still staying at Grace and Favor but was late for dinner, so Mr. Prinney made a further announcement about the library. "It appears that we've already resolved the problem that Miss and Mr. Brewster and I were dealing with. So feel free to use the room anytime you wish."

Everybody was obviously curious. But they were too polite to ask questions.

Lily changed the subject. "Dr. Toller should be here soon. He has interesting things to tell you about the skeleton. Especially about her moccasins."

"What about them?" Robert asked.

"I should let Dr. Toller tell you. But I can hardly keep it to myself. She was wearing small moccasins. They're completely intact and very pretty. He says they were probably soaked thoroughly in beeswax. Aside from a scrap of leather, and the other beads that were loose in the soil, that's the only article of clothing that survived. The beads are smaller than the other ones that were found."

A moment later, Dr. Toller arrived, apologizing for being late but proudly showing around the small shoes.

"Poor little girl," Phoebe said. "Can you tell how she died?"

"No, I'm afraid I can't," Dr. Toller admitted. "There was no sign of an injury. No broken bones, at least. It could have been a disease. Smallpox or measles. The bones don't tell me."

"She might have been one of my family," Chief Walker said.

"You're an Indian?" Toller asked.

"Only an eighth part. But the old genes were passed down."

"Do you think she was buried there before or after this house was built?" Robert asked.

"I know bones. I don't know houses. Do you know when it was built?"

Everyone looked at Mr. Prinney for an answer.

He thought for a minute or two, and said, "Mr. Horatio Brewster inherited it from his Aunt Flora. She was born around 1850, as I recall. She was known to have been born and grown up here. So the house must have been here since at least that date. I can check the records at the city hall. They might still exist."

"But she was a couple feet outside the foundation," Robert pursued. "No matter when the house was built, she wasn't dug up then, or she wouldn't have been found this week."

"I was telling Miss Brewster a little while ago that the skeleton should be preserved at a museum. Right now it's impossible to guess when she died. But someday science will figure out a way to determine this. I hope some of us survive until that happens and one of you finds out."

"I'm going to stay one more day, Mr. and Mrs. Prinney, if Miss and Mr. Brewster agree. I want to see her bones well packed into a crate. Then you can present me with your bill for feeding and housing me."

In spite of what Mr. Prinney, Lily, and Robert had discovered in the library, nobody demurred about being paid.

"I for one have enjoyed having you here," Lily said. "You discovered such interesting things. We seldom have guests as knowledgeable as you are."

On that note, Dr. Toller put the moccasins aside and began his dinner as the others finished theirs.

CHAPTER EIGHT

Thursday, April 27

DR. TOLLER had asked the Harbinger boys to make him a sturdy crate to ship the girl's bones, beads, and moccasins to the pathologist and then to a museum. He called a freighting company he was familiar with in these cases. "Do you mind if I leave her in your garage next to your car, Mr. Brewster?"

"Not at all. But let me know when they're coming so I can move the Duesie out of their way." What he really meant, of course, was that he didn't want anybody bashing his precious automobile with a rough wooden crate.

While Dr. Toller and Robert were working this out, Howard Walker sat at his desk at the jail, his feet up on the desk, eating a jelly doughnut he'd bought at Mabel's Cafe. He was thinking about the skeleton of the young Indian girl. He wondered if she, like him, was all or partly of the Munsee subtribe of the Delaware tribe, from which he, too, was descended—in a sense. His great-grandfather, a full-blood Munsee Indian, had married into a Dutch family, needless to say, to the Dutch family's disgrace. Walker was a name many of the tribe shared.

The old tribes had all had their fill of the Dutch settlers infringing on their land and way of life. They'd packed up and gone West, taking everything they owned in a wagon or on their backs. Only a few families remained. Those families who emigrated wrote letters home saying they'd changed their names to Walker because they'd walked hundreds of miles to find other tribes to join up with.

When Howard was about eight years old, his grandmother, as Dutch-looking as anyone could be, told him that when she was born, the third of six children, all of them fair-haired and with pale complexions, her own mother, when eventually widowed, decided they'd change their name from whatever their Indian name had been to Walker. Howard's grandmother told him he was her favorite grandchild because he looked so much like her own father—dark-haired with a proud handsome face, though his coloring was paler than her father's.

He'd hated his looks in grade school. The other kids called him names, making fun of him for having Indian features. The boys made jokes about where he hid his tomahawk. And was he a good shot with a bow and an arrow? As he grew older, however, he realized that girls liked him better than the other boys. He was taller, darker-haired than most of the Dutch boys, and more handsome.

That was when he came to terms with himself. He was only one-eighth Indian but had overridden those powerful Dutch genes the whole rest of his family had acquired from his tough, practical great-grandmother.

Still, he felt oddly sad about the poor little Indian girl, buried under what would eventually become huge dead bushes. What kind of life had she had? Lily had told him about Dr. Toller's theory that she'd possibly lived in a cave. At least her family had buried her properly laid out in her best clothing with all the beading on her clothes and shoes. They made sure her feet didn't get cold and wet in the winter.

As he took a bite of the doughnut, his phone rang. It was the fingerprint expert.

"Have you identified it?" Howard asked.

"No record of anything like it in the records. It's distinct, though I didn't notice it until I used the magnifying glass. It's a thumbprint, of course. But it also has a long-healed cut right up through the middle of it. Quite distinct if you look closely."

"If I happen to figure out who painted the swastika on

the tailor's shop, we'll know he's the perp from his thumbprint then? Which thumb?"

"The left. He was probably right-handed and handled the can with his left hand and rested it at some point on the window."

"It was stupid of him not to notice and clean it up," Howard commented.

"Not necessarily. Maybe he didn't have cleaning rags handy and didn't want to wipe it off on his clothes—if he even realized he'd left a fingerprint."

"Thanks for letting me know," Howard said.

The moment he'd hung up the phone, it rang again. It was Harry Harbinger. "Chief, Edwin McBride has been murdered in that shed we set up for him. Come quickly. We haven't touched him. We knew better."

Edwin was indeed dead. Dr. Polhemus was already there before Chief Walker arrived. Howard would have been happier with almost any other doctor to sign the death certificate. Howard wouldn't have even recognized Edwin except for his brown hair and plaid shirt and brown trousers, both much patched. His face was reddish-blue, his blue eyes were wide open, and his mouth was open with his purple tongue protruding as if he were still gasping for breath.

"Strangled with a fine wire," Polhemus proclaimed. "Must have died hours ago. The flesh has swollen, concealing it, all but at the back of his neck. A thin piano wire, probably."

Or some other kind of wire, Howard thought, but said nothing.

Both Harry and Jim Harbinger were seriously upset. "He was a nice, hardworking man," Harry said. "Who would do such a horrible thing to him?"

"He had no enemies?" Chief Walker asked.

"Not a chance," Harry said firmly.

"We'll have to get him to a pathologist. I know several of them," Chief Walker said. "It's clearly a murder, not an accident. First, I'm calling the funeral home in Beacon to pick him up until I can find someone to do a thorough examination."

"Be careful stepping outside," Harry said. "Jim found him and upchucked near the shed door. I'll wash it away soon."

Howard asked for permission to call the Beacon funeral home from the Harbinger house and had an ambulance around in record time. By then Chief Walker had contacted the pathologist who'd been at Grace and Favor when the skeleton was discovered.

Dr. Meredith gave Walker the address of the morgue in New York City.

The ambulance was still present, so Walker gave them the address to deliver the corpse. The guy driving the ambulance said, "I can't go that far. We don't have the budget for using that much gasoline. But there's a good pathologist in Newburgh. Could we deliver the body there?"

"What is the pathologist's name?"

The driver told him.

Walker called Dr. Meredith back to explain and ask if the other pathologist was known to him, and if he was reliable. Meredith said he knew the man and he'd do a good job.

"You'll see that I'm right about the piano wire," Dr. Polhemus said in a cranky voice. "It's obvious."

Walker ignored him and gave Harry a handful of change to pay for the calls. "Be sure to let me know if I owe you more when the bill comes." Then he asked Harry again, "Are you sure that Mr. McBride had no enemies?"

"I can't imagine him having a single one. He was such a shy man, and worked so hard at the train station. Golly!" Harry said. "Edwin was about to make a little more money there with the post office boxes. Who's going to do the sorting now?"

"Robert Brewster, I assume," Howard said. "It was, after all, his idea."

Howard was thinking furiously about where to go from here. A nice man. No enemies whatsoever. Howard's experience told him this was seldom true. Everybody had said or done something wrong to somebody else at one time or another. Mostly it was harmless and was forgotten or forgiven. But there were also people who were of a mind to take offense when none was meant. Even a well-meaning compliment could set them off.

"Did Edwin tell you anything about his past?" Walker asked Harry.

"Mostly he talked about how grateful he was to Jack Summer, who told him about Voorburg at the Bonus March. You know he came here because of Jack's description of the town?"

"That's what I'd heard," Walker said. "Anything else? Like where he grew up, or if he had family elsewhere?"

Harry thought for a few minutes. "I think he mentioned growing up somewhere in south Yonkers."

"Nothing about family?"

"Only that his mother is a really good cook."

"Did he suggest that she was still living?"

Harry shrugged. "I assumed she was because he said 'she is' not 'she was.' "

"Do you have any idea of his age?"

"No. But he met Jack at the Bonus March, so he must have served in the Great War. That would make him at least in his mid-thirties or older. I think he might have been in his early forties."

Chief Walker went back to his office and put in calls to the county records people in Yonkers. He was told they probably had the information he needed, but he'd have to hunt for it himself. Someone would help him, but not do it for him, he was told.

This would have been the perfect thing to tell a deputy to do. If he had a good deputy. What he had was only Ralph Summer, the cousin of Jack Summer, the local newspaper editor. How could cousins be so very different? Jack was sharp as a tack, and never printed anything in the *Voorburg Times* that couldn't be verified by at least two other sources. Ralph, on the other hand, was stupid and lazy. And what's more, he was currently engaged to the only daughter of a successful (so Ralph said) jeweler in Albany. Howard wondered how that had happened. Would a successful man turn over his only daughter to a lump like Ralph? Unless there was already a bun in the oven. Ralph was spending all his free time, and more, driving to Albany and was there now.

It was too late today to make the trip clear to south Yonkers. He'd leave early tomorrow to hunt through the birth and death records for McBrides. If he didn't go tomorrow, he'd have to waste the weekend.

Since he had a few minutes to spare, he called the chief of police in Beacon. Chief Simpson had a deputy he didn't like because the deputy was shy. But Howard had recently worked with the chief's deputy on a previous case and thought Deputy Ron Parker had potential. A lot more than Ralph.

"Hello, Ed," Howard said to Chief Simpson. "How's the gout?"

"Almost gone. I can get around pretty much during the day, if I wear slippers in the evening. How are things with you, Howard?"

"Not so good. My deputy is in love and will probably marry soon and move away. I'm wondering how you're getting along with your deputy?"

"Not well. And I received a letter today from an officer in Buffalo who sent his list of accomplishments and education in police work. He's so desperate to get farther south that he'd take a slight cut in pay. You want Parker? I'd really like to hire this guy from Buffalo."

"I certainly do want Deputy Parker," Walker said. "I got along with him just fine."

"I can't imagine how. The boy is bone-deep shy. When do you need him?"

"As soon as you get your new deputy. When will he start?"

"We can get this done in a day or two, I imagine. How 'bout if I tell Deputy Parker today that you want him to start next Tuesday. What's that? The second of May, I think. And I'll call my new man and tell him to be ready to start here the same day?"

"Suits me. Thanks, Ed."

Howard sat back in his chair. He'd have to fire Ralph, but he was apparently marrying into a family that might take in the newlyweds anyway. Especially if there were a baby on the way already.

As it turned out, he didn't have to fire Ralph. His deputy burst into the office moments later.

"Chief, I've got bad news for you. Jeanette and me are getting married Monday. Her father says so."

"Jeanette is pregnant, right?"

Ralph didn't even blush. "Yep. And it's not a church wedding. Just a judge and two witnesses. Her own folks. So I can't invite you."

"That's okay."

"Sorry to leave you in a lurch."

"I'll get by," Howard said with a smile.

"I've got to go pack all my stuff. Like I said, I'm really sorry."

The moment the office door closed, Howard called his former landlady. "Have you rented both my old rooms yet?"

"Not even one of them," she said in a surly voice.

"Then I can help you out with one of them. The one with the phone connection. I'm getting a new deputy next

Tuesday. Will you arrange to have the phone reconnected by then?"

On Friday when he drove to Yonkers, there were a great number of McBrides listed in the birth certificate files, but only one Edwin. Born in 1899, mother Sharon McBride. No father listed. So he was probably born out of wedlock. Not that it mattered. At least they knew his age. Walker checked for a death certificate for Sharon McBride and came up with nothing. He then searched in the city rosters in Yonkers and found her address given five years earlier. He found the house but Sharon McBride no longer lived there. A friendly neighbor told him where she'd moved.

Much as he hated giving anyone such bad news, he felt obligated. Sharon McBride turned out to be much older and more shop-worn than he'd imagined. Her gray hair straggled out of a red-and-white handkerchief tied around her head. She smelled of lemon oil.

She took the news badly.

"Poor little Edwin. He was such a nice little boy. Very popular in school. Why would anyone murder him?"

Walker had felt obligated to tell her the truth. If she saw her son's body, she'd know it wasn't a natural death. "That's what we don't know. When was the last time you heard from him?"

"Oh, dear. Several weeks. But I've had so much cleaning up to do in this place I hadn't got around to giving him my new address yet."

"Do you have a cemetery plot for him?"

"Yes, I bought two. One for myself and one for him."

"Is your husband there already?"

"There was no husband. He bolted when he learned I was pregnant. That's why Edwin has my maiden name."

"We'll see to sending his body for burial when the pathologist is done. I'm really sorry to be the bearer of such bad news."

"No. Don't be sorry. I needed to know this. Otherwise I'd have never known what became of my son."

CHAPTER NINE

MRS. MCBRIDE seemed to be hanging on to her emotions by a fine thread. She'd removed the kerchief from her head and made an effort to fluff her hair up a bit. Her face had gone pale. It was all Walker could do to keep himself from hugging the old woman to show his sympathy.

But when she'd pulled herself together and insisted that they have coffee and cookies, he agreed.

He was glad that there would be somewhere for McBride to be buried. But he wasn't any closer to knowing who had killed him and why. Before he left Sharon McBride's house, he asked about Edwin's friends when he was a youngster. In his own experience, bunches of boys were always led by either a good-natured boy or by a bully. Edwin was obviously the former. But there was almost always a "hanger-on" who was a younger brother or just somebody who attached himself to the group without invitation.

Girls, he was told, were different. The prettiest was always the leader. And she always had a "best friend" who was homely, to show up how pretty the leader was. He'd always wondered if the homely girl had a crush on her mentor, or disliked her but didn't want to lose her place in the group.

He'd asked Sharon McBride if she still knew the boys Edwin went around with.

"Oh yes. Most of them are still in the old neighborhood."

"Could you give me their names and last-known addresses?"

"I can. Most of them still drop in and visit me from time to time, to talk about the old days, and they send me Christmas cards."

This shift in the conversation seemed to bring the color back to her face. "I have their addresses." She rose and opened a drawer in a buffet table. But as she fingered the pages, her hands shook. She handed the book to Howard. She gave him the names to look up, and he wrote them down.

"Was there a 'hanger-on' as there always seems to be?"

"Of course. His name was Mario Scalia. I don't hear from him."

"Do you think he's still in the old neighborhood?"

"I have no idea. The other boys might know, though."

The last thing Walker had to tell Sharon McBride was that the coffin should be closed because Edwin didn't look good and she wouldn't want to see him that way.

She thanked him for telling her.

He thanked her for the addresses and said, "If you need me I'm on the telephone exchange in Voorburg."

She hadn't cried until then. "Oh, my poor baby," she sobbed. Howard put his arm around her shoulders and said, "Everybody in Voorburg liked your son. We'll miss him. Let me know when the funeral is taking place and I'll be there."

He'd have to interview all of Edwin's old friends. But it could wait for a day or two. Sharon McBride said she wanted to tell his friends that Edwin had died, before Chief Walker did.

When he returned to Voorburg, he also heard from the pathologist in Newburg that Dr. Polhemus was wrong—as usual. It wasn't piano wire, it was a long section of wire that jewelers used to saw through rings that had to be cut off fingers when knuckles had swollen too much to remove them. Howard's first thought, which he was ashamed of, was that Ralph Summer was about to marry the daughter of a jeweler. That wasn't fair to Ralph, probably just coincidence.

Lily, meanwhile, knowing nothing about the death of McBride yet, was thinking about archaeology. Unearthing that skeleton, while tedious, was very interesting. Knowing about rickets and living in a cave were revelations she'd have never guessed. The beading and beeswaxed moccasins were also fascinating.

She knew she was good at bookkeeping from her experience working with Mr. Prinney on estate matters. Maybe she could also be good at something else. There was no way she could attend college, however, to learn more. Great-uncle Horatio's will clearly stated that neither of his heirs could be away from Voorburg for more than two months a year, and they must make their own living in Voorburg. Obviously there wasn't a college in Voorburg. They were lucky to have a grade school. She'd have had to move into a dormitory somewhere else, which wasn't an option.

She wondered if there was a way to take classes by mail and only go in for tests a couple times a semester. How could she find out about that? Oh, she thought, almost slapping her forehead. At the town library.

Miss Exley was an expert in researching almost anything. She would certainly have reference books, however outdated, about colleges.

Lily gave Miss Exley a warning call about what she needed.

"I might be able to find something. I'll start with Vassar," Miss Exley said. "Just because it's the closest to you. But I doubt they care about educating women to be anthropologists."

"Probably not. Certainly some school in New York City would know. And I think I can find the telephone number of an anthropologist who might know where they have a course by mail, so I'd only have to go to the city to take tests."

"Why are you suddenly interested in this, if I may ask?"

"Haven't you heard about the skeleton we found at Grace and Favor?"

"No. Who was it?"

"A young Indian girl."

"Oh, how sad to die young. I'm afraid I've been too busy still working on getting all the old newspapers in order to read recent ones."

"I don't think Jack Summer has reported it yet," Lily said.

Miss Exley said, "I will watch for his next issue. I'm beginning to fear it's going to take me the rest of my life to get the old newspapers in order. And I've decided that anyone who wants to see a newspaper has to read what they find in front of me, so I can stop them if they try to cut out an article. You have no idea how many of the newspapers look like grubby lace."

She went on, "If you can wait until tomorrow, I'll be glad to see if we have any books here on the subject that are less than fifty years old. But I can see why you're interested. Meanwhile, if you give me the town where your source of information is, I can look him up in the most recent New York City telephone book."

"I think we have a fairly recent one somewhere at home," Lily said. "Let me try that first. I hate to put you to that much trouble and expense."

"Do you really want to be an anthropologist?" Miss Exley asked.

"Not exactly. For another reason, I couldn't go out in the field and investigate finds for another eight years anyway. Our great-uncle's will demands that we make our living for ten years without being out of Voorburg more than two months of any year."

Miss Exley said, "I'd heard two women checking out romances talking about that, but I chalked it up to plain old gossip. It's really true?"

"It is. But I'd just like to get more information."

When she got back to Grace and Favor, she called Dr.

Toller's office but was told by a receptionist at the college in New York City that he was out of the office for the day. But she'd give him the message to call Miss Brewster back. He'd mentioned to her when he'd returned from Voorburg how interested and useful Miss Brewster had been by helping with the successful excavation of the skeleton.

•

Chief Howard Walker assumed that Mrs. McBride would call on Friday or Saturday the other "boys" who'd been pals with Edwin. Howard would try to find as many of them as he could on Sunday, when they were most likely to be home. It was a shame he wasn't getting Deputy Parker until the next Tuesday. It would have been good for the young officer to sit in on the interviews. He managed to find all of them at home, and one of them even knew where the "hanger-on" currently lived.

He couldn't help being surprised that all of the "boys" were older than he. But to Mrs. McBride they were still nice children who'd happened to grow up.

CHAPTER TEN

MONDAY, MAY FIRST WAS LILY'S BIRTHDAY. Robert had gone early in the day to fetch the books he'd left with Mrs. Smithson.

"I assumed that a man who doesn't know how to make coffee also doesn't know how to wrap packages either," she said with a smile. "I had some extra birthday paper and the books are all wrapped and ready and back in your box."

Robert grinned. "Your guess was right. I was going to ask our maid or Mrs. Prinney to wrap them for me. It was kind of you to save me from more embarrassment."

Not only had she wrapped each book individually, but the paper was lovely and each package had a ribbon tied in a fancy bow.

Howard Walker had come home early and asked Mrs.

Prinney for a small vase of water, which he carried out to the woods behind the mansion, picking a big handful of the prettiest wildflowers he could find.

Phoebe Twinkle had made a pink felt hat with a very stylish brim and embroidered flowers around the crown.

Mrs. Tarkington had wrapped up a small bracelet another teacher had given her years earlier and that Lily had admired. She'd told Lily at the time, that while it was pretty, it wasn't really her style.

Mrs. Prinney had prepared a good-sized pork roast (most of which would serve as leftovers and sandwiches for Phoebe and Mrs. Tarkington for lunches), mashed potatoes with thick, tasty gravy, sliced tomatoes she'd put up in jars last summer, and a fabulous three-tiered chocolate cake with one candle on it.

Everybody sang "Happy Birthday" as Lily blew out the candle. Robert disappeared for a moment to fetch the books that he'd hidden in Mr. Prinney's office, and he set them at the corner of the table. Lily eyed them while she opened Phoebe's box and put on the hat. It fit perfectly. She thanked Howard for the flowers. She was already wearing Mrs. Tarkington's bracelet and thanked her again, then asked, "What are those other four packages?"

"They're from me," Robert said.

"And you wrapped them yourself?"

"Of course."

Lily raised an eyebrow.

"Okay," Robert admitted, "Mrs. Smithson wrapped them. She's been hiding them at her house."

Lily smiled. Opening all four in a row, she gushed, "Oh, Robert. My favorite four authors. How did you know?"

"I pay attention to what you read." Then realizing he couldn't get away with this either, added, "Miss Exley made the choices. All I did was go to the city and buy them."

Lily was almost choked up by the gifts. "Thank you, everybody. Mrs. Prinney, that was a wonderful meal. Phoebe, this is a gorgeous hat, and the flowers are lovely, Howard. Mrs. Tarkington, how nice of you to remember how much I like this bracelet. This has been the best birthday I've had for years."

"Don't get weepy about this, Lily," Robert pleaded. "I hate it when you cry."

She dabbed at her eyes with the table napkin and said, "I'm sorry to be sappy."

Mrs. Prinney and Mimi started clearing the table. Mr. Prinney went back to his office, claiming he had letters he needed to get out on tomorrow morning's train.

"Speaking of the mail train," Robert said to Lily, Phoebe, Mrs. Tarkington, and Howard, "I hear that our very own chief of police is telling people I should run this post office thing in the station."

Howard nodded. "It was your idea. It's pretty much up to you to pursue it, don't you think?"

"I've thought about it and you're right. But I don't want to do it forever."

"Do you have someone else in mind?" Lily asked.

"Not yet. But I'll keep an eye out for someone else to take over. If it happens, of course. I need to get back to getting people to sign the petition and present it to the town council for approval. Lily and Mr. Prinney need to give me some guidance on what the costs will be, and how much should be charged for a box, and how much of the money should go back to the city for funding it."

"That should be easy to compute," Lily said. "We could work it out tomorrow, so you can get started with the petition."

Phoebe had to excuse herself. "I have two hats that aren't quite finished and both ladies want them tomorrow."

"And I have lesson plans to work on. I have a teacher out tomorrow going to the dentist and I have to fill in," Mrs. Tarkington said, likewise excusing herself.

When the two lady boarders had departed, Lily said, "I'm expecting more books to arrive soon. I spoke to Dr. Toller. I explained that I'd like to know more about anthropology but couldn't leave Voorburg to study at a college."

"Why can't you?" Chief Walker asked.

"I thought you already knew. Almost everyone in town does," Lily said. "According to our Great-uncle Horatio's will, we have to earn our living for ten years here in Voorburg. We're only allowed to be somewhere else for two months a year."

"But if you wanted to go to college and could get a grant or something, wouldn't that count as the 'right' thing to be doing?" Howard asked.

"It should be," Robert said. "But it would go against the conditions of the will and Grace and Favor would never be ours. Or at least not Lily's if she was gone for months at a time."

"And Mr. Prinney enforces this, I assume?" Howard queried.

"He has to. It's his responsibility to make sure we fulfill the conditions," Lily explained.

"So that's why he and his wife live here?" Howard was still trying to get a complete understanding of this weird inheritance.

"It's one reason," Robert said with a laugh. "Another is because Mrs. Prinney loves to cook for all of us."

"I still don't see how it's fair," Howard said. "Getting a good education is important."

"It's not a matter of fairness, Howard," Lily protested. "It was the conditions we agreed to two years ago. It's why we're always scrambling for some sort of income. And to tell the truth, I don't really want to be an anthropologist. I just want to know a little more about it. That's why Dr. Toller is lending me some first-year textbooks."

Lily thought it was time to change the subject. "I understand you were gone all day yesterday, and Ralph Summer has gone missing."

"Not really missing. He got married last weekend. And had to move to Albany."

"How are you going to do all you have to do without a deputy?" Robert asked.

"I won't be without one. I've snagged one from Chief of Police Simpson from Beacon. He wanted to replace him with a guy who was desperate to get out of Buffalo."

"Why?" Robert asked. "Not that anyone in their right mind would stay in Buffalo, I hear. They say it gets more snow every winter than any other city. But if this young man he's sending you isn't good enough for another chief of police, why would you want him?"

"Because he has more potential than Ralph ever did," Howard replied. "A bit shy, but better educated than Ralph, and he really wants to be in law enforcement. You'll like him. He's a nice young man. I had Deputy Parker with me when I was up there in Beacon about the body in that horrible lake. You might remember him.

He's the one who rushed that typewriter to be fingerprinted a month ago."

"Where were you all day Sunday?" Robert asked. "I tried to call you."

"What about?"

"I don't remember," Robert said with a laugh.

"I'm the one who's supposed to question people," Howard said with mock seriousness. "As a matter of fact, I was in Yonkers questioning Edwin McBride's old boyhood friends."

"Do you think one of them had a grievance against him that bubbled up suddenly decades later?" Lily asked. "That would be a good trick for a mystery writer to use."

"In a way," Howard said. "His mother told me that there was a boy in the group that hadn't been invited and didn't fit in. She knew where the others lived, but not where he was. So when I interviewed the others I was curious to see if any of them could lead me to him."

"And did they?" Lily asked.

"You're still plotting, aren't you?" Howard asked.

"Just curious." Lily almost blushed at his perception.

"Okay, I'll give you the story." He didn't think it would be right to give their surnames. "I started with the 'second-in-command,' a man named Dennis, who looked as if he, his wife, and three kids were all from Scandinavia. Tall, blond, and healthy. He praised Edwin to the skies.

Said he was both funny and honorable. He told me that Edwin wouldn't let them do things they shouldn't. He found interesting things to do. Circuses. Block parties, even if it wasn't their own block. He even forced them to go to a couple of museums. When Edwin was unavailable, Dennis took over. But he didn't know where the 'hanger-on' was.

"The second was a Patrick. A musician. Currently playing trombone for dance marathons. He hated them. They put people through hell for the chance of winning very little money. Men and women both fainted from exhaustion. Of course, the bands changed. Each of them did only six hours a day. He didn't even remember that there was an extra person in the old gang."

"This sounds as if they were all nice people," Lily said. "Not good suspects."

"The fourth one wasn't quite as nice, if that makes you feel better," Howard said.

"Oh, good. Tell us about him."

"Fat, sour, unhappy, sloppy, and cranky. Jake, he was called. He'd been married three times and all of his wives had left him. Still, he was loyal to Edwin, Dennis, and Patrick. They'd been good friends and if they'd all stayed together he wouldn't be in this mess."

"Please tell us that he knew the 'hanger-on,'" Robert begged.

"He did. I found him in a seedy office a few blocks away. His name was Mario. He probably has no home and sleeps in the back room of his office. I suspect he has grown-up gang ties and keeps a very low profile. His desk was magnificent, but the chair he offered me was in tatters. When he heard that Edwin McBride was murdered, he laughed. Said he deserved it. He was a Goody Two-shoes. Claimed he hadn't seen or heard from him in many years."

"You got a fingerprint, didn't you?" Robert asked. "I'd like him to be the perpetrator."

"Why would he be, except that he didn't like Edwin? But I did get a fingerprint anyway."

"How?" Lily asked.

Howard looked a bit embarrassed. "I bought a big white cup that was spotlessly clean. And I'd only touched the handle. "As I was leaving, I asked if he could fill it. There was a pot of coffee brewing on a table. He told me to help myself, but I faked a sudden cramp in my calf and shoved it near him."

"Brilliant," Robert exclaimed.

"Not brilliant at all. Sheer good luck. He picked the cup up in both hands and filled it. I sent it off for fingerprints this morning."

CHAPTER ELEVEN

Tuesday, May 2

IN SPITE OF Robert's thinking getting a fingerprint on a coffee cup was brilliant, Howard knew that the most he could find out was whether Mario, the last man he interviewed, had a criminal record. He was unlikely to have anything to do with Edwin McBride's murder. Not after all those years had passed.

It was remotely possible that Mario knew Edwin lived in Voorburg. Jake had been in touch with Mrs. McBride and she knew where her son was. Jake could have told Mario. Jake must have been occasionally in touch with Mario to know his office address.

But the fingerprints wouldn't be useful as a key to the swastika painted on Mr. Kurtz's window. That was a completely unrelated crime.

Meanwhile, Howard was looking forward to the arrival of his new deputy, Ron Parker. Walker had made Ralph leave his uniform behind. Ralph was hard on clothing. The Voorburg police budget had had to cough up a new uniform a mere three months earlier. Ralph's old uniform would be too long in the trousers, and too fat around the middle for Parker, but Mr. Kurtz could get it to fit properly. Ralph hadn't had time to get stains and snags on it.

Parker took the train and arrived just after noon. He was wearing his old uniform, which really didn't fit him well either. And the patch on the sleeve identifying him as an officer in the Beacon Police Department could be replaced with Ralph's old one.

Walker asked, "Have you had lunch yet?"

Parker hadn't, so Walker took him to Mabel's. Somehow she'd found good hamburger somewhere and they both stuffed themselves on sandwiches, fried potatoes, and green beans. There was also a pudding. But it had been made with dried milk instead of the real thing and was bland and lumpy.

Parker, thin and fair-haired, kept his eyes on Walker while they ate. Ron Parker was still astonished that Chief Walker, his idol, had actually wanted to hire him.

After lunch, he took Parker to Mr. Kurtz to refit Ralph's uniform to Parker's slighter stance and replace the patch on the sleeve when the jacket was done. Walker then took his new deputy to his office in town and told him what little he knew about Edwin McBride's death. He explained that he'd already interviewed McBride's old gang of friends and his one enemy. He invited Parker to go over the notes he'd taken.

"I don't like the sound of this Mario guy," Parker said. "Couldn't Jake have told him where McBride lived?"

"He could have. But I doubt it. Jake must have known that Mario held a deep dislike of McBride. I doubt that the dislike was enough to send him up here after so many years."

They left it at that for a while, and Walker told Parker about the swastika on Mr. Kurtz's shop window.

"Whoever it was had stolen a can of red paint and a brush from Harry Harbinger's backyard," he told Parker. "And then stupidly returned the can of paint but not the brush. I managed to find an expert to lift the fingerprint he made with his left thumb. It was very distinct because of an old cut in his thumb."

"He or she? Sounds more like what a discontented old woman would do," Parker speculated. "A woman who's been abandoned by a husband or cut off from her children and turns nasty to everyone."

Howard was quiet for a moment. "That could be true. I just assumed it was a man." Ralph would never have thought about that. And frankly, neither had Howard himself.

"Why would anyone paint a swastika on a newcomer's place of business? He didn't sound German to me when we were in his shop," Parker asked.

"He speaks English well because he was born in St. Louis to a brewer and his wife. They spoke German in their bar, since most of their patrons spoke German. But spoke English at home. In fact, Robert Brewster says that Kurtz's granddaughter got him out of Germany in the nick of time. A day or two before the German police started forbidding foreigners from leaving Germany."

"Who is Robert Brewster?" Parker asked.

"Darn it, Ron. I'm explaining this too fast. Of course you don't know him. Or rather, remember him. It was his sister Lily who got that typewriter a month or two ago. You were along and rushed it to Newburg."

"Oh, yes. At least I remember Miss Brewster. A really pretty woman. I'm not sure I'd recognize her brother."

"I'm now a boarder at their mansion," Walker told Parker. "It's called Grace and Favor Cottage. Soon I'll invite you to a dinner there so you can get to know the people who live there. I'll also introduce you to other people in town. As far as I'm concerned, you'll be here for a good long time and need to know about the people who live here."

Ron Parker almost blushed with pleasure at this complimentary comment.

Howard went on. "Speaking of boarders, I've arranged for you to live for the time being where I used to live. There's a phone line I had activated. You won't like it anymore than I did. The whole place reeks of cabbage. But when you get to know the town better, you can probably find something nicer. Mrs. Smithson, Mr. Kurtz's granddaughter, owns lots of property in town. Most of it vacant. But you'd have to cook for yourself. Do you know how to cook?"

"I sort of know how to make a sandwich. I never lived in a place that had a stove after I left home."

"You'll have to learn to cook," Walker said. "Or spend your whole income on eating at Mabel's. My housing and yours come out of the police budget, paid weekly by me. I'll take you and your suitcase to the boardinghouse now. There are three girls who handle the telephone exchange. You'll soon recognize their voices. Two don't listen in. One does. You can wait for the sound of a click of the operator hanging up when you're connected. If you don't hear it, tell the operator it's police business and to hang up."

Parker almost reeled as they entered the boardinghouse. "What's that awful smell?"

"Old cabbage. It permeates the entire house, all the furniture, all the bedding. You'll have to put up with it until we find you somewhere else to live."

Howard led him upstairs and opened the door to the room that Walker once used as his bedroom. He'd also had a second room as his office, which was now vacant. "I'm afraid there aren't locks on the doors. If you have anything valuable, I can put it in the safe at my office in town."

"Only my billfold and a few family pictures. I keep my billfold in my pocket and can put the pictures on the nightstand."

"Nobody will steal them."

Howard was close to gagging. He'd never realized, until he escaped the boardinghouse, how the old cabbage smell seemed to collect upstairs. It was bad enough in the front hall. Upstairs it was worse.

He suddenly felt terribly guilty about doing this to Deputy Parker.

"Let me call Mrs. Smithson. It's only mid-afternoon. You haven't had to eat here yet. Mrs. Smithson owns a lot of property that she inherited. She might have somewhere you could live instead of here."

Parker grinned with relief.

Mrs. Smithson was at home and free for the rest of the afternoon. "Why don't you pick me up in the police car? I've never ridden in one." She said this in what was nearly a girly giggle.

She directed them to a place a bit out of town first.

The house was small and empty. Even on a nice day in May, it smelled musty. There was no stove or icebox. No furniture at all. The only things that remained were dishes, glasses, silverware, and pots and pans.

"The police department is responsible for housing a deputy. But I can't afford to furnish this. And it's quite a way from town," Chief Walker said.

"I see," she said. "Let's go back to town. I have a second-floor set of rooms your deputy might like."

This was much better. It was the second floor of the greengrocer's shop. Mr. and Mrs. Bradley had lived there for years, and they'd finally decided when their daughter and son-in-law wanted to stay there with them that they'd have to move out and find a house. There wasn't room for more than one guest, and then there was the baby to account for. The Bradleys were going slightly mad with all three of them living on cots in the living room and keeping him and his wife awake half the night. The baby was colicky and cried all night. So they moved to a small house close to town, and helped their daughter and family find another even smaller house.

There was a large bedroom, a kitchen with a stove, icebox, and a nice big table. Also, lots of empty cabinets. But there were no plates, glasses, silverware, or cooking utensils.

Apparently, Mrs. Smithson's late husband had owned

the building, Walker assumed, since she appeared to be authorized to rent it.

Mr. Bradley said, "When we moved, I carted out my wife's three sets of dishes, the glasses and silverware, all the clothing, and the pots and pans. I wasn't about to strain myself hauling out the bed, or that big kitchen table and the sofa. We also left the bedding."

"That empty house we looked at first had pots and pans, glasses, dishes, and silverware. Remember?" Mrs. Smithson said. "Apparently the former tenants thought it was all too heavy to go in their car when they started out for California. You might have to get some good scrubbers and soap to clean them up, but you're welcome to them, Deputy Parker. If you drop me at home, I'll give you the key. You can return it when you've collected what you need."

On the way back to Voorburg after collecting the dishes, glasses, pots and pans, and silverware, Ron Parker asked his boss if the landlady at the boardinghouse was going to be angry if he left without even staying overnight.

"Of course she will. But I've already paid for the first week," Walker said. "So it's not that she didn't make a little money. Remind me to ask the phone exchange to disable that phone line and activate the one in your apartment."

Walker dropped Parker off to reclaim his suitcase and

family pictures and waited in the police car. They delivered everything to the apartment, and Walker went to Mrs. Smithson's home to return the key. "Here, take this to your deputy when you can," she said, handing him a book titled *The Boston Cooking-School Cook Book* by Fannie Merritt Farmer.

"Don't you want it anymore?"

"No. My mother gave me this old copy, and later a friend gave me a newer copy with a lot more recipes. This one is simpler and will be less complicated to understand for someone who's never cooked. He lives right above the greengrocer, after all. It's not too hard to find food there. He even carries bread, sugar, flour, and coffee and tea. He'll have to go to the butcher down the block for meat though. And if there's anything else he desperately needs, he can find it in Newburg."

Walker went to visit Parker that evening. "Do you have a suit?" he asked.

"An old brown one. It's in fair condition. Why do you ask?"

"We need to go to Edwin McBride's funeral. For his mother's sake, and ours, we need to see who turns up, try to eavesdrop on them. See if some clue I haven't found yet drops into our laps."

"How was he murdered?" Parker asked.

"Strangled. With a wire that had fine projections that dug into his throat."

Parker frowned. "That's nasty. But not as nasty as that other case we worked on."

"Not quite," Walker said. That case was more horrible than any Howard had ever known about. A boy had been pushed into a disgusting lake in early winter and didn't float to the top until the spring thaw. Howard had taken Parker along to interview neighbors and to see the lake. It smelled so nasty that it made both of them gag. Walker had forced Parker, who had been terribly shy then, to conduct one of the interviews himself. Parker had done a good job. A much better job than Ralph could have pulled off. It was the reason he'd wanted Parker when he thought he'd be likely to be rid of Ralph. Parker could be brought along and he'd learn to get over being shy.

"When is the funeral? I need to shake out the suit and spruce it up. And I also need to buy a tie."

"I can loan you a tie. And I don't know when the funeral will be yet. But I'll give you fair warning when McBride's mother tells me. We don't want to show up in police uniforms. And give me the brown suit. Mimi, the maid at Grace and Favor, can make it look almost new."

CHAPTER TWELVE

HOWARD WALKER was awakened at three in the morning when his phone rang. It was Mrs. Smithson.

"We've had a fire here at my grandfather's shop."

"Is the fire out?"

"Yes."

"Don't touch anything. Call John Butler. He's the head of the volunteer fire department. I'll be there as soon as I can."

He threw on his clothes and ran into Robert in the hallway. "Where are you going at this time of the night? I heard your phone ring," Robert said.

"Fire at Kurtz's shop."

"I'll follow you."

"All right, but don't interfere," Howard said as he ran down the stairs.

Mrs. Smithson met Walker in front of the shop. "Grandpa's really upset."

Howard looked at the metal trash can tipped over on the sidewalk. It was charred and on its side. And there was water on and in it.

"Grandpa smelled smoke and opened the front door," Mrs. Smithson said. "The can was leaning against the door and almost fell into the shop. He kicked it away and came back and poured a pitcher of water over it. Then tipped it over. The awning over the front door was also burning. He ran up the stairs and poured another pitcher over it. I've told him to sit and rest. I was afraid he'd have a heart attack."

She'd thrown a coat over her nightgown and parked her car a few feet away from the shop. She was shivering even though the night was warm.

"You need to rest, too," Walker said. "I'll have the can examined by an expert in fingerprints and someone who's an expert in arson by morning. Are you sure the shade over the door isn't still smoldering?" he asked, looking up.

"Dear God!" she exclaimed, looking up as well. "There is a wisp of smoke coming off the top."

Howard ran inside, asking Mr. Kurtz where he'd left the pitcher.

"In the bathroom upstairs," Mr. Kurtz said in a shaky voice.

Walker found and filled the pitcher and called down, "Mrs. Smithson, stand away from the building."

When he could see her out in the street, he poured three pitchers full of water on the shade. Meanwhile the volunteer firemen and Robert Brewster appeared. "Don't touch anything," Walker shouted from the upstairs window.

Lights were going on in houses on the next block. People were coming out to gawk. A moment before Robert showed up, Ron Parker had come running at the sound of the fire truck. He'd thrown a coat over his pajamas and was still wearing house slippers.

"I'm glad to see you, Deputy Parker," Walker said. "Help me to keep everyone away from this trash can. Someone leaned it against the front door and set it on fire. It's evidence of a crime. No, Robert! Don't touch the trash can!" Walker added.

Parker said, "Give me five minutes to put my uniform on, would you, Chief?"

"I'll watch it until you're back. I need to question Mr. Kurtz as soon as I can," Walker replied.

"Is there anything you want us to do?" John Butler asked Walker. He was already rolling the hose back up on the ancient fire truck.

"Go home and catch up on the missed sleep," Howard said.

As the firemen left, Robert asked, "Want any help? I came around the corner and saw you upstairs at that window pouring water over the canvas shade. Want me to make sure it's safe now?"

"I'd appreciate that and so would Mr. Kurtz and his granddaughter."

When Parker returned, dressed in his old uniform, Walker said, "I have two people to call in the morning as soon as I can. You're going to have to sit out here all night, I'm sorry to say, to make sure nobody touches the waste bin."

"I'll stick around for a little while to keep you company, Deputy," Robert offered. "May I go inside and try to find a chair for the deputy to sit in?" he asked Mrs. Smithson.

"I think there is one in the basement," she said. "Now I'm going home. I feel silly standing around in my nightgown, even with a coat over it. I'll just make sure my grandfather is sleeping before I leave."

Robert, meanwhile, went to the dark basement, felt around the door for a light switch, and found the chair in question. It was a rocking chair with a pad tied to the seat and the back. He wrestled it up the stairs and out the front door.

"Here's something you can sit on, Deputy. The cushions, I'm afraid, stink of mildew."

Parker said, "I don't need cushions anyway. I might be too comfortable and fall asleep. Thanks for dragging it up here."

He settled in, sitting forward alertly. Robert leaned against the windowsill and said, "You might not remember me, but we've met before."

"I recognized you when the chief called you Robert. You're the one who hauled out the typewriter."

"I am. But credit goes to my sister for getting it as far as the front porch. Could I bring you a book to read, or a pot of coffee and a cup?"

"Too dark to read," Parker said. "But coffee would be good."

Robert took off in the Duesie and headed up the long winding road. He looked in the kitchen for a recipe book that would tell him how to make coffee, eventually figuring out that Mrs. Prinney didn't need recipes. She had all of hers in her head.

He made the best of a bad situation. The old stove was still barely warm enough to heat a pan of water. He put another piece of kindling into the stove. While it was warming up, he rummaged in the pantry to find the coffee. There should be directions on the package. There were none, so he guessed and put a half a cup of grounds in the tepid water.

As he pulled the pan of water and ground coffee off

the stove, he realized he had to strain it somehow. He looked in all the upper cabinets, then the lower ones, where he eventually found a strainer. The holes were fairly big, so he used a dishcloth in the bottom, thinking how very clever he was.

He found a clean milk bottle waiting outside to be replaced, presumably by a milkman at some point in the future. He washed the bottle, carefully poured the coffee into it, wrapped it in a whole wad of dishcloths, and took it to the car.

He was about to start the Duesie when he realized he hadn't thought to put the cap on the bottle. What if it tipped over and spoiled the leather seat? He contemplated holding it between his knees, but he wouldn't be able to use the brake, gas, and clutch if his knees were together. Finally he settled for grabbing an old jacket from the backseat and tying the sleeves around himself and the bottle. It was uncomfortably warm, even in spite of the dishcloths padding it.

As he pulled up in front of Mr. Kurtz's shop, he saw that Mrs. Smithson was back, wearing a pair of trim trousers and a short-sleeved blouse. She was handing a thermos to Deputy Parker.

Robert hopped out after untying his jacket and himself from the now tepid bottle and said, "I brought coffee."

"I thought you didn't know how to make coffee? That's what you said before," she said. She took the bottle from him, sipped at it, and choked. "Oh dear! This would keep any normal person wide awake for a week. Not to mention how gritty it is. You come over to my house tomorrow afternoon and I'll teach you how to do it right and where to buy a thermos."

Robert thanked her in a thin, cold voice and added, "I'll do that."

A block away, he dumped the coffee out of the milk bottle at the side of the road and went home to bed.

When Howard Walker returned the next morning with his consultants, Chief Colling from Newburg, and a fire marshal he'd brought along, Deputy Parker was slumping in the rocking chair, holding one eyelid open with his finger.

"Go home, Ron. You look half-dead," Chief Walker said. "Get some sleep. I can handle this myself today unless something else turns up."

Parker tried to rise from the rocker and nearly toppled over. Walker caught his arm. "It's not far. Can you walk?"

"Barely," Parker said bravely, stretching out one leg and then the other and setting out for his new lodgings over the greengrocer's shop. He didn't look as if he'd make it the two blocks without falling down.

Walker said to the other two men, "It's his first day on the job and I left him to guard the can overnight."

Both men laughed.

Chief Colling asked, "How did you get rid of the dumb lump of a deputy you used to have?"

"I didn't. He got a girl from Albany pregnant and had to marry her and live with her family."

"Happy Families," the fire marshal said with a wink. "Now let's look at this trash bin." He put on a pair of fresh white cotton gloves and held the sides toward the bottom and turned it upright. "Probably no fingerprints in this area," he added as he leaned carefully into the bin and took a deep breath, then stood up. "No fire starter accelerator. No gasoline or kerosene smell. But plenty of dry wood. It looks like slats from cartons of some sort. Most people would keep it for kindling. Unless they already had too much kindling."

Deputy Parker staggered in the door of the greengrocer's shop.

"What's wrong with you, boy?" Mr. Bradley asked. "You look like a wrung-out rag."

"I was babysitting a trash can overnight," Parker said.

"That's probably mine," Bradley said. "I went out early this morning and it was gone."

"Do you mind calling Chief Walker and telling him that? He'd like to know."

But when Bradley called, Walker already knew. He said, "We found an invoice for a crate full of apples in the can. I'm sorry I can't return it yet. I have to hold it for a day or two to have it fingerprinted. It's a bit charred."

"Charred?"

"Someone set fire to the packing slats in the trash bin and then leaned the bin against the front door of the new tailor's shop."

"That's awful!"

"More than awful. It's arson and attempted murder," Howard said.

CHAPTER THIRTEEN

ROBERT WAS GOING AROUND TOWN with his much-revised petition to build a mail sorting center at the train station. So far he had twenty signatures. He was approaching Chief Walker next and found him in his office in town, with his feet crossed on the desk and his chair tilted back.

"You're going to kill yourself someday sitting that way. The back feet will slip and you'll crack your head on the windowsill."

"Maybe so," Howard agreed. "But this is my deep-thinking position, and I have some serious thinking to do right now."

"About the fire last night at the tailor's shop?"

"I've been thinking that it was a man who did both the swastika and the fire. He's an avid hater of Germany. But my new deputy suggested that it might be a nasty old woman. That had never crossed my mind."

"Could an old woman have carried that trash can from the back of Mr. Bradley's grocery shop?" Robert asked.

"The crate slats weren't that heavy, and they were all dry because we've had so little rain. And the can wasn't completely full. A strong woman of any age could have carried it by the handles."

"No word yet on fingerprints?"

"Some. I called the expert who got the painted fingerprint and asked if it was necessarily a man's. He said he couldn't tell. It wasn't a small woman's but some men also have smallish hands. He hasn't had time yet to check the trash bin though. But if that same fingerprint is on it, we still don't know the sex of the person."

"Nor do we know if it's somebody local, I'd guess," Robert said.

"I've been thinking about that, too. It's likely, I'm sorry to say, it's someone who lives here and knows their way around. But there are also frequently people who turn up in Voorburg thinking they might find jobs. Those who don't have a car or train fare, and probably camp out in the woods in good weather like this."

"What about that old enemy of McBride's that you interviewed in Yonkers?"

"Nope. His fingerprints didn't match. And it's a

whole different crime. But I can't imagine what a German hater would have against a man named McBride," Walker went on.

"Are you absolutely certain of this?"

"I'm not absolutely certain about anything at this stage," Walker said, suddenly angry. "I've never been so completely ignorant of any crime before. I usually have a few obvious suspects. Even when none of them are actually guilty. But questioning people almost always leads to other suspects, one of whom is usually guilty. This time there's almost nobody to question. Not even one witness has seen the person threatening Mr. Kurtz. No one saw anyone who had reason to murder McBride. Two cases on my plate. Both distasteful."

"I haven't any advice for you, but one of those old women who was raking through everybody's mail that day I was there could have lifted a small car off its wheels. She had arms like ham hocks and pudgy fingers. Deputy Parker might be right—that a woman could have hoisted that trash can with one hand."

"But painting the swastika on the window first?"

"She—if it's really a woman—is as likely as a man to hate and fear Germans these days. She probably has no reason to believe he was born in America."

"I'll keep that in mind," Howard said. He sounded halfhearted to Robert. But Howard had been asking for an opinion and Robert had given him one that was possible. Maybe not likely though.

"How's the petition going?" Howard was obviously changing the subject.

"Pretty well. I have twenty people who signed it just today. I'm seeing more of the townspeople tomorrow and the next day, then going out in the countryside to convince the farmers."

Robert thought about Howard as he went around town collecting signatures on his petition. At least Robert had a plan. It wasn't as exciting as murder and attempted murder, but he still believed it was important to have a place to sort the mail so the snoops couldn't know what other citizens were receiving.

He went to see Mrs. Smithson for his coffee lesson and took the petition with him. It turned out that making coffee wasn't all that complicated after all. It was just measuring water and coffee in the right proportions.

"Would you like to sign the petition to set up a little post office sorting room at the train station? Read the introduction and then I'll tell you why I think it's important."

When she'd finished reading, Robert told her about the old ladies examining other people's mail and deciding who should get certain letters and which they should destroy.

"I've seen them doing that," she said. "I think it's disgraceful. How will it be set up?"

Robert explained about the numbered boxes people could pay for and put their own lock on, if they wanted to. He also told her about the little room behind it with the box numbers and an open space.

"So who is going to do this?" she asked, sipping the coffee Robert had made himself.

"Well, right now I'll be stuck with it. I was trying to get Edwin McBride a paying job. Of course that won't happen now."

"It's so sad about his death. He was a nice man. Always polite and helpful. Does the chief of police have any suspects?"

"I have no idea," Robert lied. He didn't want anyone else to know how upset Howard was about having no good leads in either of the current crimes.

Jack Summer approached Mrs. Smithson, asking, "May I ask your grandfather for an interview yet? We have two new residents of Voorburg. Your father and a new deputy. People here need to know about both of them."

"Of course. But I'd like to be at the interview with my grandfather."

They both went over to Mr. Kurtz's shop. He was busy taking in some of his own granddaughter's dresses. "I'm paying for these," Mrs. Smithson told Jack. "I've lost a lot of weight recently. The trip to Germany took it off. Grandpa, this is Jack Summer, the editor of the local paper. He'd like to ask you about your new business and a bit about your background."

"I'd be glad to converse with him. It will perhaps bring in more business."

"I understand you left Germany to come to Voorburg. How did that come about?"

"I was afraid of living in Germany. I'd once had the misfortune to attend a Communist meeting where we had to sign in with our names and addresses. The Nazis hate the Communists as much as they hate the Jews."

"Mr. Brewster told me you got out of Germany just in time."

"Yes. My granddaughter and I didn't realize it until we got here. The German police were about to refuse to let Americans leave the country."

"Are you an American, too?" Jack asked.

"I was born and raised in St. Louis." Mr. Kurtz went on to explain about his father being a brewer who took his family to Germany.

"Is anyone else in your family still there?" Jack asked.

"No, my parents died a long time ago. My only sister, much younger than I, came back to America ten years ago and lives in Arizona. I hope she'll come to visit us soon."

"Why did you take up tailoring instead of being a brewer like your father?"

"I didn't really like being a brewer, so I apprenticed myself to a tailor when I was a young man in Germany. He taught me well. He had many customers as the economy faltered and I gained a lot of experience. I put away everything I earned working for him, and when my apprenticeship was done I acquired the best tools I could find. I must admit that Germany makes the best tailoring tools in the world. I knew I'd want to eventually return home and wanted to have the best shears and needles."

"Is your business going well so far?"

"I suppose you could say so. I've been here a short time and have had four customers already. Including my granddaughter," he said, smiling at Mrs. Smithson. "She's a good girl to come and save me from the Nazis."

Jack asked, "Is there anything else you'd like our citizens to know?"

"Just make sure they know I was born in this country. I'm a full American and love this country."

When Jack had put his notebook back in his pocket, he thanked both of them and departed. Mrs. Smithson said, "Grandpa, you said exactly the right things. I'm so proud of you."

"And I'm proud—and grateful to you, sweeting."

CHAPTER FOURTEEN

JACK SUMMER'S next visit was to Howard Walker's office. "Chief, do you know anything more on McBride's death that I can report in the *Voorburg Times*?"

"Nothing I can report about yet."

"Anything about the person harassing Mr. Kurtz? I just interviewed him. He's a nice old guy."

"Nothing to report yet," Walker repeated. "Any other questions?"

"Two more questions. First, I'd like to talk to your new deputy. It's not often we get two new reputable people living in Voorburg."

"If you don't mind, he had a long night guarding that trash can. I sent him home to sleep. How about tomorrow?"

"All right. He'll be in the next week's first issue instead of this week's last."

"What's the other question?" Walker asked.

"Do you know anyone who has a car they'd like to sell me?"

"What's wrong with the motorcycle with the side car?"

"Well—" Jack looked a bit embarrassed. "It's this—" Jack was actually blushing. "Mrs. Towerton invites me to dinner about every two weeks."

"That's nice. Does it include anything more than dinner?" Howard asked with a smile.

"Not yet. Her children eat with us, and then she puts them to bed, and we sit out on the front porch in good weather and drink lemonade. Winters, we sit in the kitchen and drink hot chocolate. But I'd like to pay her back. A really good dinner at a good restaurant. She could get a neighbor to take the children for an evening. But I couldn't possibly take her in the sidecar of the cycle. It would blow her hair and clothing to smithereens. I need a car. Know anybody who'd like the motorcycle? Maybe in kind for a car?"

"The only one I know who needs a motorcycle is my new deputy. But he has no car to trade."

"Would the police budget allow you to buy it?"

"Nope. But maybe Deputy Parker could pay you in installments and I could kick in a buck or two when it's available."

That afternoon, Robert found Lily reading a book in the library. The French doors were open and there was a nice warm breeze. She looked up from her book. "It's spring, Robert. I thought it would never come again."

"What are you reading? One of the books I bought you?"

"No. I'm spacing them out. I don't want to gobble them all up at once. This is one of the books Dr. Toller lent me. First-year anthropology. It's interesting. Just the basics."

She set the book aside and asked, "How is the petition going? Have lots of people signed it?"

"Thirty-nine so far. I hope to find another twenty before submitting it to the town council."

"I haven't signed it yet. Find me a pen. Is Mr. McBride willing to be the unofficial postman?"

Robert was temporarily speechless. "Didn't you know? He's been murdered."

Lily gasped. "Why has nobody told me this? I don't know him well. I've only seen him when I take Mr. Kessler's little carved animals to New York to refresh Jimmy Anderson's supply and collect my royalty on the sales."

"You're still doing that? I never noticed you being gone for a day," Robert admitted.

"That's because I don't mention it much. I only go to the city every six months. Mr. Kessler has increased his supply. And Kessler's carvings are getting better and better.

"Who killed Mr. McBride? And why didn't you tell me about this?"

"Howard doesn't know who did it yet. And I didn't tell you because I thought everybody in town knew about McBride's death. Jack Summer mentioned his death in his last newspaper. I thought you always read it."

"We're both supposed to since we inherited the *Voorburg Times*, but I've come to trust him. Why hasn't Howard mentioned this? After all, he lives here," Lily said.

"His job isn't the subject of dinner talk, Lily. And we don't own the police department. It's just like you don't mention Mr. Kessler's carvings."

"How was Mr. McBride killed?"

"Strangled. In that little shed the Harbinger boys fitted up for him to sleep in. Dr. Polhemus swore it was a piano wire. I'm glad to say he was proved wrong. It was a long strand of wire that jewelers use to cut off rings when they can no longer go back over a knuckle."

Lily turned pale. "I'm sorry I asked. Sorry, too, that I didn't know. Did he have a family?"

"Yes, a mother who bought cemetery plots for both herself and her only son. Howard told me this."

"I suppose that's a good thing. Did we inherit cemetery plots? Our mother and father are buried in one. Did they buy two for us?"

"Golly, Lily, how would I know? Or want to know?"

"Who's going to take the job of sorting the mail?" Lily asked.

"Unfortunately, it's me. But just if and when the sorting area is built. I don't want to spend my life doing this. And I don't really need to."

"Wouldn't you be paid something?"

"I would. That's why I don't want the job," Robert explained.

"Are you crazy?"

"Lily, we're okay financially. We made a lot of money on those awful people who stayed here when their kingpin was murdered. Then there are those fake books. Lots of people need a job worse than we do."

"But it's what Great-uncle Horatio specified that we had to do. Earn our own living," Lily objected.

"Great-uncle Horatio has been dead for years."

"But Mr. Prinney isn't," Lily said. "And he's responsible for making sure we earn our own living."

Robert opened his mouth to speak, then changed his mind. What he'd been about to say was that Lily was merely sitting around reading while he was busy trying to get enough signers on the petition to create a place to sort mail.

He knew this wasn't fair. Lily worked with Mr. Prinney most of the time sorting out matters of the estate. Collecting rents on properties that could pay them. They often gave some of the companies and farms the estate owned permission to miss a payment or two in order to keep going. She more than paid her way. If he had to do what Lily did, he'd go insane with boredom.

"I'm off to see if I can get a few more signatures. I thought I'd hang out at Mabel's cafe."

It turned out to be an even better idea than Robert anticipated. He got there at four-thirty and stayed until eight, when Mabel's closed. He sat at a table at the front of the shop and explained what the petition was about. He collected twenty-two more signatures, including one from one of the nasty women who had been interfering with the mail. Apparently, she herself was illiterate and only commented on what the other two told her. She signed with an X and Robert had to ask her name and put it down, saying it was her mark.

Her friends, if they found out, would be furious.

Tomorrow he'd consult privately with the town treasurer to see if the town council would meet and let him explain what had happened that caused him to circulate this petition.

Around the same time Robert was entering Mabel's, petition in hand with several pens, in case one ran out of ink, Howard was taking a phone call.

It was the fingerprint expert. He sounded as if he were delivering a present. "Easy as pie, Chief. The same thumb that was on the window is also on the trash barrel. Now we have the whole set of prints on file. Every single finger."

Howard wished he could be as thrilled as his informant. But he made a good pretense of being excited by the information. Both the swastika and the attempt to burn down the building were done overnight. Did that mean the person was local? Did he (or she) know where everything in Voorburg was? Would a stranger know where to find a can of red paint? Or a trash can full of dry slats? Probably not.

Perhaps, though, it was someone from a nearby town who had cause to visit often. Maybe somebody who had a grown child or children living in Voorburg and visited often.

He wished he could fingerprint everybody, but that wasn't possible or even legal. He'd have to have just cause to fingerprint anyone, although he'd fudged the law by tricking Mario.

Still, knowing there was a record of all of the perpetrator's fingerprints was reassuring. He wouldn't have to depend on the man or woman leaving a single left hand thumbprint, if there was another attack on Mr. Kurtz's person and safety. He was glad Jack Summer had interviewed him for the local paper. That might stop the perpetrator, knowing that Mr. Kurtz was an American returning to his own country for fear of the Nazis.

He hoped that would stop whatever prejudice had led to the insult of the paint and the more serious attempt to burn down the building with Kurtz inside.

It didn't help, however, in finding out who'd succeeded in the horrible murder of Edwin McBride.

CHAPTER FIFTEEN

Wednesday, May 3, and Thursday, May 4

LILY HAD GONE TO BED early with her textbook on anthropology. Her dog, Agatha, thought it smelled interesting since so many people had handled it when reading it. She had to keep pushing Agatha away. "I'm glad my sense of smell isn't as good as yours. Though how you can think a long-dead animal smells good enough to roll in defeats my imagination."

She eventually fell asleep with the book on her chest and Agatha sprawled on her feet.

Thursday morning, after breakfast, she and Robert remained behind to chat.

"Does Jimmy Anderson, who has that expensive gift shop in the city, still call himself the Duke of Albania?" Robert asked.

"Of course. And I address him as such in case a customer is in the shop."

"How does this work? I don't think I'd trust him an inch to be fair," Robert said.

"We agree on a reasonable price for each piece. He can add his profit to that, I take my meager commission out of the reasonable price and pay back the remainder to Mr. Kessler. What Jimmy and I agree is 'reasonable' is quite a high price to begin with because they sell so well."

She went on to tell Robert about Agatha smelling her well-used textbook because it smelled like so many other people. Then she asked, "Did you get a lot of signatures last night?"

"More than twenty, including one of the old bats. She apparently can't read or write so she signed with an X."

Lily laughed out loud. "She just goes along for the other ones to read the return addresses? So what happens next?"

"I made an appointment to talk to the town treasurer and show him the signatures and explain the rest."

"What is the 'rest'?"

"That the Harbinger boys will make the letter boxes with scrap wood, but will charge for the work. Then they install hardware—which the city also pays for—that will hold combination locks. Customers buy these for themselves. We then buy duplicate numbered coupons that the first two hundred people sign up and pay a dollar for."

"Who gets the money?"

"Well, I do at first. But I have to give half of it back to the city treasurer. Then once a year, everybody who wants to keep their box, pays another dollar, and again half goes back to the city. If somebody doesn't get enough mail to make it worth it, and wants to give it up, whoever is sorting gets to resell the box for the full price and keep all of it."

"Sounds complicated to me."

"Not really. The sorter makes half the money up front, and half each year, the whole amount if somebody gives up a box. And a meager payment back from the city every month."

"So there's actually money to make at the job?"

"Up front, of course. Not so much as it goes on. But I've been thinking of saving half of whatever I make when it goes into business, then give the other half to whoever takes over from me," Robert explained.

"Who are you considering passing the job to?"

"Maybe that Susan person who works at the movie house selling tickets. She probably would make more money on this for less work and wouldn't have to get her sister—who raises rabbits—to take care of Susan's kids every night."

"So it would be a day job while her kids are in school? What a good idea. Did you really think this all out for yourself?"

"Well, I had a little help from Howard and Harry Harbinger. And I ran into Mrs. White, who asked about it after signing, and she suggested Susan Gasset. By the way, is that ladies' group still going on?"

"The Voorburg Ladies' League? Yes, but it doesn't meet as often as it used to. Mrs. White had to give up the idea of the trading truck going around to houses. It was too complicated to compute what equaled what else. Especially for foods that got old fast. We only meet every other month now and make things for the poor. Blankets, quilts, winter gloves, and two in the group are experts at knitting woolen socks for every size. It's a bit hard to get excited about it in nice weather like this. But by winter we'll have a good supply."

"I must go," Robert said, consulting his watch. "My appointment is at ten and I want to be early."

At dinner that night, Robert bragged, deservedly, on his coup. "First, I told the treasurer why I'd become interested in this. About the old ladies going through other people's mail and speculating if one person's mail should be destroyed before she saw it. The treasurer was appalled."

"So he should have been," Mrs. Tarkington said.

"Then he started asking me questions about what it

would cost and what percentage of the profits should be returned to the town council—if any. I thought that remark boded well. I never expected he'd not automatically demand reimbursement."

"Maybe he feels that the town council is truly responsible for the welfare of Voorburg residents," Lily said.

"He'd fund the grade school more generously if he felt that way," Mrs. Tarkington said. "We're teaching with old books that we keep having to paste back together. They're all out of date."

"Then you take up a petition, too," Robert said.

"I may do so. It seems to have worked with you," Mrs. Tarkington said, realizing too late that she'd offended him.

Mrs. Prinney spoke up. "What's the next step, Robert?"

"The treasurer is calling a special meeting of the whole council tomorrow. He wants me there to explain to them what I told him."

"Doesn't anybody else get to help make the decision?" Howard Walker asked. "Shouldn't there be some sort of public meeting? After all, the town council receives the money they can dispense from public taxes."

"I don't know," Robert admitted. "We didn't talk about that. You may be right. I'll make a note to myself to ask that tomorrow."

Robert had one more piece of information to find before the meeting. He went to locate Harry Harbinger to find out what Harry and his brother Jim would charge to construct the boxes, what the hardware would cost, including their fee for putting it on.

"I've been thinking about this. We're talking two hundred boxes, tops. The labor for it I'd estimate at a week, plus another day or two to get the hardware and the sorting table inside installed. I'd need the cost for the hardware to be paid in advance. I'd estimate thirty dollars for labor and ten for the hardware, maybe five for the sorting table, door lock, and labor. If it's less, I'd settle on the actual cost."

"That sounds reasonable to me," Robert said. "It's a lot of work."

He wrote it down in the notebook he'd bought. Ten up front for hardware. Thirty for labor, five for the table, door, and lock.

Robert was early for the meeting. It was held at the dining room table in the treasurer's house. The treasurer, Peter Winchel, a man who was at least fifty and had a very deep voice, was already at the head of the table, going over the notes he'd made of their earlier conversation. And other questions and suggestions he thought of and anticipated.

"You're a bit early, Mr. Brewster. It's good that you

are. Are you prepared to tell us the cost of building the sorting area?"

"I am, sir."

"And the estimated time it will take?"

"Yes."

"Another thing I want to bring up," Winchel said, "is what to call it. I don't think we can call it a post office. The real postal system wouldn't like it. So we'll need to talk about a different title for this project, if the rest of the council approves it."

"I'll give this some thought. Do you think it's going to be approved?"

"I'm fairly certain it will. I want you to be ready to tell what you saw and heard that made you bring this to our attention. The women going through everyone's mail and don't forget to mention the woman who said that someone else's letter should be destroyed for her own good. Don't name names, of course."

"I don't know their names anyway."

The other four members were prompt. A Mr. Horsely was the secretary and opened his notebook, and laid out a pen and inkwell. He was a thin, scholarly-looking man, probably in his forties. Next was a big, scowling man who looked a bit like a bulldog, with a projecting lower jaw and mottled red, freckled flesh pushed up by his tight collar. He was introduced as Arnold

Wood. "What's this all about?" he barked as he took his place at the table.

The treasurer said patiently, "All will be explained when the rest are here, Arnold."

The other two joined them the next moment. Men in their fifties wearing rather shabby clothes, but pleasant expressions. Robert learned these were Todd Taylor and Jake Wilson, who had a cobbler's shop in town.

"Gentlemen, this is Mr. Robert Brewster, who lives up on the hill at Grace and Favor. You may already know him."

"The boy who drives the fancy big yellow car all over the place." Arnold Wood sneered.

Boy? Robert thought, but kept his face from showing his irritation.

The treasurer ignored this remark, and proceeded. "Mr. Brewster and Mr. Buchanan observed something going on at the train station that they've reported to me that needs attention. I'll turn this over to Mr. Brewster to explain."

Robert stood up. He felt he'd have a better presence that way. He told, briefly and unemotionally, about the three women going through everyone else's mail, which was in sacks on the floor, and making personal comments, including one about a certain woman in town. She had received a letter with a return address; they thought the letter shouldn't be delivered because it was from someone they didn't approve of. They had debated destroying it. At that point, Robert was called away to the train that was arriving with a package for him. "I don't know if they destroyed it or not," he said in an effort to be fair.

There was silence except for an audible gasp from one of the cobblers.

The other cobbler said, "That's horrible. What can we do about it? I don't have any guilty correspondence, but I wouldn't want to have three old bats pawing over my mail!"

"Nobody would," the secretary said, as he was writing down what Robert had reported. "May I ask a question?"

The treasurer nodded.

"Does this happen regularly?"

"I've only observed it once. But the stationmaster, Mr. Buchanan, says they do it almost every day. You can check this with him, if you wish."

The treasurer said, "Mr. Brewster figured out how much this would cost and has a floor plan to show you. He's also consulted with local workers, Harry and Jim Harbinger, about the cost. I'll let you explain this, Mr. Brewster."

Robert did so. He passed around copies of the plan, showing the area behind the boxes, the worktable, and the locked door. "The station, as you know, is enormous. It won't crowd the seating area or the booking area. The boxes will be open at the back and customers will pay for their own locks. The hardware to attach these locks is included in the bid from the Harbingers."

Everyone agreed that it was not only a good idea, but a reasonable price.

Mr. Horsely asked, "How long would it take?"

"The Harbingers say two to three weeks. Closer to two. But they want to allow for three," Robert informed them.

"Now, there's a question or two I have," the treasurer said. "Mr. Brewster and I already touched on this. We can't call it a post office. We need to think up another name."

"Letter and Package Center?" Mr. Horsely suggested.

There were nods to this and a vote was taken. Only Arnold Wood abstained from voting.

"The second thing is this," the treasurer went on. "Mr. Brewster has what I consider a somewhat elaborate plan for paying the person who does the sorting. I won't bother you with the details. My suggestion is we decide how much work this job will entail, how many hours it will take, and what would be a fair amount of financial reimbursement for whoever does the work. In return, I'd recommend that a very small percentage of the cost to the customers to rent the boxes, and for the lottery tickets to acquire a box, be reimbursed at five percent up front, but only for long enough to cover our initial investment, then the annual cost of the box should be set by us, and the sorter pay us the same percent as a town tax on the property."

Again, the group agreed and voted. This time Arnold Wood voted with the rest of them.

"One more question, Mr. Brewster," the treasurer asked. "Who's going to do this?"

Robert smiled and said, "Chief Walker suggested that I do it, because I started this, but I don't need the job right now—"

Arnold Wood butted in. "Chief Walker! The man's an incompetent. Why, he doesn't even know yet who killed that man McBride. We need a new chief of police. He's always slow on the job."

Robert couldn't resist this jab. "That's probably because he always waits until he has proof of who committed the crime instead of just accusing someone."

"Sure, you'd say that. He lives in luxury, I hear, at your mansion. Great pal of yours. Do you know who he suspects?"

"We don't discuss his job over the dinner table, sir," Robert snapped. "He's a boarder just like the milliner and the principal of the grade school and we don't question them about their jobs. It's none of our business, or yours, for that matter." Robert turned to the treasurer and said, "To get back to the subject at hand, I thought about asking Mrs. Susan Gasset if she'd like to take the job. She's the cashier now at the movie theater, and it's a long hard day for which she's probably paid a pittance, and her children seldom see her. Her sister takes care of them. This would be a day job while the children are in school. I haven't approached her yet, and would prefer to get her opinion before we decide."

"A girl doing a job that should go to a man?" Arnold Wood shouted.

Robert said, "Mr. Wood, do you have any idea how many men have run off and left their wives to cook and take care of the kids? How many women have done that? None that I know of."

"Arnold, shut up," the treasurer said, standing up, red in the face. "Mr. Brewster is right. In my experience women are smarter and harder working than men anyway. Furthermore, none of them here in town have run out on their families like so many men in town have done. You are the rudest man I've ever known. I'll accept your resignation, if you'd care to submit it. Meeting adjourned until Mr. Brewster talks to Mrs. Gasset."

Everyone fled the meeting as quickly as they could, leaving Arnold behind.

"Bastards. All of you," Arnold shouted.

CHAPTER SIXTEEN

ROBERT'S NEXT STOP after the meeting concluded was the train station. "Mr. Buchanan, could you tell me how many mail trains come in on any given day?"

"Three. One at seven-thirty in the morning. That's the biggest since most of the mail comes from New York City overnight. Normally three bags. Then the noon one is usually two bags. The last one of the day is at four and it's almost always one bag. But there is no delivery on Sunday at all. So each Monday morning is commonly four bags."

"That's interesting. I wouldn't have guessed. How big are these bags?"

Mr. Buchanan brought one out of his office to show Robert.

"I thought they'd be huge. But they're not. Thanks for the information."

When he returned to Grace and Favor, Robert called Susan Gasset's house, introduced himself again because they'd talked the day before when she signed the petition, and asked if she'd be interested in a new job.

"Am I ever!" she exclaimed.

"Could I spin by your house and have a talk with you this afternoon?"

"Come to the theater. There's a matinee today. I have to be there at one. By one forty-five I'm free, but have to be back in the booth at quarter of four for the four o'clock people, and then for the eight o'clock showing."

"You have to just hang out there the whole time between movies?"

"I have to total up the tickets and match it to the money. It takes me a half hour at least and more if it's a big crowd."

"Do you go home between?"

"Sometimes I do. When one of the kids is sick and out of school. I don't want to put my sister to more trouble than I have to."

"We'll talk about this on one of your free times today. Okay?"

"That's fine. Nobody's sick today," she said with a laugh. "How about two in the afternoon?"

While Robert waited around to meet with Mrs. Gasset, he stopped by the jail.

Howard said, "What now?"

"Do you know there's a nasty man on the town council who wants you fired?"

"Yep, I've heard that. Old Arnold Wood. He used to have a very profitable bakery up Route 9 a little way. When the drought hit the Midwest he couldn't get enough flour at a good price to keep it up and had to shut it down. Had to give up his big house and move to a little one. He and his wife have a son living with them. A complete lout. A big fat boy who hates dogs. He goes around kicking them whenever he gets a chance. He's killed a few of them. A few of the bigger, cannier ones have snuck up on him later and bit him in the back of the calf or thigh. The last time I heard, three of them had sent him to the hospital to get stitched back up and have rabies shots."

"Why does that make Arnold Wood want you fired?"

"Because he wants to get the kid out of his house, and to take over my job."

"Fat chance!"

"I know. But he will never give up on it. He's desperate to get the obnoxious kid a job."

"The treasurer of the council got so mad at him for being rude to me and criticizing you that he asked him to resign."

"He was rude to you as well?"

"Because he called me 'the boy' who drives around in

the Duesie, and he didn't like it that you live at Grace and Favor. And what's more, you haven't found somebody to blame McBride's death on yet."

Howard put his head in his hands. "I'll bet that fat son of his could have found someone to blame—without any reason—by now. He knows nothing about police work and is universally hated. Especially by people who had the little dogs he killed. There would be a full-fledged revolution in Voorburg if he got the job. Still, it's damned annoying of Arnold to keep harping on me."

"I guess you couldn't get his fingerprints with the coffee cup technique?" Robert said with a laugh.

"I couldn't. I'd need a warrant and you can't get one just because someone is obnoxious and rude."

"But, Howard, he and his son are the types of men who would be perfectly willing to have killed McBride just to put you in a bad spot."

"Not really. Arnold's all bluster. He wouldn't do that. The son might. If he can kill dogs, what's to stop him from killing a person he didn't like. Frankly, I don't think he'd have the courage. He usually picks on little dogs."

Robert looked at his watch, and said, "I've got a date with Mrs. Gasset on her break."

"A date?"

"More of an appointment. I want her to take over the mail sorting if it comes about, as I hope it does."

Mrs. Gasset was sitting on a bench across from the theater. She didn't notice him at first, and Robert studied her for a moment. A pretty woman a year or two older than he. But sadly, she had three children and a rather terrifying sister, Bernadette, who raised rabbits and sold the fur and meat. Robert crossed the road, sat down next to her, and said, "This is very nervy of me, but I have to ask. What do you make taking tickets and sorting out how many were sold?"

"A dollar and a half a day," she admitted.

"I think I could get you a job that's just as boring but that would earn you more money. And you could go home and spend the evenings with your family and children."

Her eyes went wide. "What kind of job?"

"Sorting mail into boxes at the train station. But not just yet. However, I really think the town council is going to approve it. What's more, you'd get a percentage of what the boxes cost. A big percentage, in fact."

"Why don't you do it yourself?" she asked. "I've signed your petition. You ought to be the one making the money."

"My sister and I make enough money to get by. We taught at the grade school for a while. We take in boarders who pay to live at Grace and Favor. Three of them so far. And room for more if everybody who currently lives there likes them. If even one disagrees, they don't qualify."

He didn't and wouldn't ever mention the cash in the

fake books to anyone but Lily and Mr. Prinney, who already knew.

"I'd be honored to take the job, if it works out. Meanwhile, I'll go on taking tickets. The owner of the theater won't want to lose me, but I would like to be at home in time for dinner and have the evening free every night. I always drag myself home around nine in the evening and the kids are already in bed."

She smiled and said, "My sister would like it, too. She says it's the hardest part of taking care of kids."

No wonder, Robert thought. *Bernadette probably puts them to bed the way she puts the rabbits to bed. Just shove them in bed (or a cage) and walk away.*

Robert went back to Grace and Favor and called Peter Winchel, the town treasurer. "I've spoken to both Mr. Buchanan and Mrs. Gasset since the meeting. Mrs. Gasset is very anxious to take the job. Could you consider paying her two and a half or three dollars a day?"

"That's up to the whole council to decide. I'm fairly sure they'd agree to two and a half, though."

"How about this—Mr. Buchanan says the heaviest day is Monday because there is no delivery on Sunday. Could you persuade them to pay three dollars for Monday and two and a half for the other days?"

"Sounds good to me," Mr. Winchel said in his deep voice that indicated his authority.

Howard heard early Friday morning from the fingerprint expert from Yonkers. "This is Joseph Cline."

"Nice to hear from you."

"I've been a bit tardy. My wife just had our first baby. But I do know about the prints on this cup. Having his full name helped a lot. I've just looked him up. Clever of you, Chief Walker, using that smooth cup. Do you want it back?"

"No, thanks. What do you know about Mario Peck?"

"First, that Peck isn't his real name. His real name is an Italian name with lots of vowels. He's a petty crook. A long list of scams. Did a little time for one that destroyed the finances of an elderly lady. Most recently . . ." Mr. Cline seemed to be trying to stifle a laugh. He went on, "Mario hit a parking meter in a borrowed car. Claimed he'd driven a long way and fell asleep at the wheel."

"Was it really borrowed or stolen? Let me guess. Stolen, right?"

"Of course stolen. But there's more to the story. He was wearing protective glasses, heavy headgear, and thick leather gloves. Behind the parking meter was an Italian restaurant where a bunch of Mafia guys were having dinner at a table at the front window."

"He was aiming for them," Howard said. It wasn't a question.

"Apparently the protective glasses foiled him. He missed his target because he couldn't see the parking meter. No real harm was done to anyone. It wasn't followed up, just entered in his record. Except for the damage to the stolen car. He did have to pay for that in trade for jail time. Shortly after that, he took that dreadful office. Laying low, apparently."

"When I went to his office and did the coffee cup trick, I noticed that his name wasn't on the door of his office. Just that it was Room 3B. Is he a known member of the Mafia?"

"It's probably part of some really low-ranking group trying to get their feet in the door with some other big guys. If Mario had done what he intended to do, he'd have done time. But come out golden. A good attorney would have been paid for by his cronies and he would have had the grateful thanks of some other big-time mobsters."

"Interesting," Howard said with a laugh, but then turned serious. "But not much good for the case I'm investigating."

Mr. Cline asked what the case was about, and Howard explained.

"That's really sad. A poor veteran down on his luck and murdered so viciously. If you do find even a remote connection to Mario, please let me know. I'd like to help, and if I can do anything for you, I'd certainly be willing to."

"Thanks. I'll keep in touch if I need to. Boy or girl? Your new baby?"

"A ten-and-a-half-pound girl. We're thinking maybe she'll turn into a good football player someday if they ever let girls play."

"What's the baby's name?" Howard asked.

"Ellen Marie."

"A lovely name," Howard said. "I'll send her a 'girl' toy."

"No need to. My wife has three older sisters who only have boys and have bought all the girly dresses and toys. Our baby's room is full of them."

"I'll send one more anyway," Howard said.

CHAPTER SEVENTEEN

Saturday, May 6, to Monday, May 8

AS WALKER HAD PROMISED, Parker's brown suit looked almost new by the time Mimi was done with it. She'd patched a fraying spot on an elbow with part of the hem of a trouser and pressed the suit to perfection.

Howard had alerted the telephone exchange that both he and his deputy would be gone for several hours that afternoon and if anything needed attention desperately to call the police in Fishkill or Cold Spring to fill in.

As they drove to Yonkers, Parker asked, "Why is this funeral so delayed? Didn't the victim die quite a long time ago?"

"Yes, but his mother had recently moved and had lost track of which box the deeds to the two lots were stored in. Poor Edwin has been on ice at a funeral home."

"Poor guy. Why are both of us going?"

"Because I need to be supportive of his mother and you need to eavesdrop at the grave site and later at Mrs. McBride's house to listen to what his friends are saying."

The funeral was well attended by his old friends. Dennis, the closest to Edwin, brought along his oldest son. The only one missing was Mario, which wasn't a surprise.

Howard wondered why, since Edwin had served in the Great War, there wasn't a military presence. He should have had at least six men in Army uniforms in attendance, even if they couldn't fire a final salute as the coffin was lowered. He supposed Mrs. McBride hadn't known she could have sent him off that way.

Mrs. McBride managed to hold herself together well with only a few tears when she threw a handful of dirt on the coffin. Howard filled the back of his car with the flowers to take back to the house.

Mrs. McBride had already made friends with her new neighbors and two women were there with casseroles, bread and butter, salads, and desserts. They left as the funeral party crammed into the small house. In spite of being in suits instead of uniforms, Walker and Parker still looked like The Law. While Walker set out the flowers on tables and the fireplace mantel, Parker moved around the room introducing himself. After dessert was finished and Dennis's wife was helping Mrs. McBride put away the leftovers, Walker and Parker made their farewells to Mrs. McBride.

When they were back in the car, Walker asked Parker if he'd heard anything interesting.

"I don't know if it's relevant, but that tall Swede Dennis was telling one of the others that he'd gone to Voorburg to visit McBride some months earlier. McBride had written to him, asking him to visit him at the train station."

"Well, well. He didn't say anything to me about that," Howard replied. "But I hadn't thought to ask when they last met in person."

"Dennis was saying how bad he felt for Edwin. Wearing old clothes, aging so much. He took Edwin to lunch at Mabel's and bought him a good meal and paid for it. He even forced a couple of dollars on him to buy some new shirts. Edwin seemed happy to be in Voorburg and had made some good friends."

Howard thought about this for a while. "I wonder if Edwin also mentioned an enemy? He probably didn't even know he had one and wouldn't have mentioned it anyway."

Deputy Parker said, "I was a little surprised to hear about Dennis visiting. But I think it just means that Dennis was a loyal friend."

"I think you're right," Howard said.

After a weekend of soliciting more signatures for the mail project, Robert dropped in at the jail Monday with his petition and asked the chief of police, "Want to sign this?"

"I sure do." He wrote his name clearly so it would be legible.

"Arnold Wood is every bit as nasty as you said," Robert declared. "When I suggested Susan Gasset as the postmaster—or postmistress—he went haywire. So many men are out of work, he said, that the job should go to a man.

"I stomped on him by saying it's the men who have all run off to greener fields, not the women, who stay home, cook, and take care of the children. Winchel backed me up and told Wood he could easily be replaced on the town council because of his rudeness. Wood blundered out saying what bastards we all are."

"That doesn't surprise me in the least. Poor Serafina."

"Who is Serafina?"

"Arnold's downtrodden wife. Portuguese, I think. At least she's from Massachusetts and there are a lot of Portuguese there. In spite of the fact that wheat and corn flour ran short because of drought in the Midwest, she found a source in South Carolina for rice flour and barley flour, wherever that's grown. While Arnold and his fat kid are sprawled out listening to the radio, she's in the kitchen making rolls that she takes to Mr. Bradley, the greengrocer. Though why he's called 'green' I have no idea. He sells all sorts of things, from bread to toothpaste and postage stamps. He can only sell her rolls if he puts a bit of icing on them, they're so bland. Or so he says. Serafina must have been a beauty in her day. She's heavy now, but she has the most elegant small hands I've ever seen. How did I wander so far from the subject?" Howard asked with a laugh.

"What about the guy you fooled with the coffee cup? Were his fingerprints on file in Yonkers?"

"Sure were. He's a small-time thief, who got in trouble for running into a parking meter in a stolen car."

"How could that happen? Didn't he see it?"

"He was dressed for a crash. Protective glasses, heavy headgear, and leather gloves. Apparently the glasses deceived him."

"What do you mean?" Robert asked.

"He was aiming for the window of an Italian restaurant where a bunch of Mafia guys were eating at a front table."

Robert roared with laughter. "Not good planning! Did he go to jail for it?"

"No, but he had to pay for the damage to the car before it was returned to the real owner."

"So you don't think he had anything to do with Edwin McBride's death?"

"Fingerprints don't match the one on the window or the set on the trash can."

"That's a pity. You could have solved at least two crimes against Mr. Kurtz."

"But not Edwin McBride, which was really a nasty murder."

Walker changed the topic. There was no point in talking about Edwin's murderer until he had some idea who it was.

"How's the mail thing coming along?" he asked Robert.

"Just fine. All that remains is to have Peter Winchel draw up a few contracts. First, with the Harbinger boys, and second with Mrs. Gasset. Then everything will start."

"How long will it take?"

"Harry thinks they can complete most of the important things in two to three weeks or a little longer. A few things, like painting, might not be completed, but the mail won't be pawed through."

"Robert, you've done a good thing. And you doggedly pursued it. Everybody except the nasty old women will be grateful to you. Maybe they should name the place the Robert Brewster Letter and Package Center."

"Golly, Howard! That would really be great."

"I'll suggest it to Peter."

Walker had meant every word of what he'd said. Robert had noticed a problem, asked around about how to solve it, found out from various people how his project might work, and was finally going to get it done properly. He did deserve the credit.

Whereas Howard himself was still at sea on two different crimes committed about the same time. He didn't even know if he was looking for a woman or a man. Although, he doubted that there was a woman responsible for choking Edwin McBride to death with a wire that almost nobody but a jeweler would own. The only jeweler Walker had ever heard of was Ralph Summer's new father-in-law. And there was certainly no reason for someone from Albany to come all this way for the purpose of killing someone he was unlikely to have known.

On the other hand, Ralph's father-in-law might know something about other legitimate reasons for needing the same sort of tool. A wire with very fine, sharp teeth to cut through things. A woodworker, possibly. Or somebody who crafted glass works. He might contract Ralph and ask the father-in-law for other suggestions. He leaned back in his chair, propped his feet on the desk, and said to himself, *no*.

He didn't want either Ralph or Ralph's in-laws to

know how desperate he'd become. It was simply a matter of his pride, but so be it.

Now that his reflections had thrown up some admittedly feeble suggestions, he was a little bit encouraged. Where and how would a normal person find a jeweler's fine cutting wire? A hardware store? A jewelry store? Maybe some sort of machine used such a thing to cut through something like cheese or bread.

Bread.

Arnold Wood. Arnold Wood's nasty son.

Arnold used his mouth as a weapon. And the only two times Howard had seen Serafina at Mr. Bradley's she'd worn short-sleeved dresses. She had smooth arms with no sign of bruises. But the son was truly violent. So far as Howard knew, his violence was only toward dogs. But could he have murdered a person?

How in the world could he possibly prove this?

And how would the kid have even known who Edwin was? Edwin was at the train station or in the Harbingers' shed all the time. According to what Howard had heard about Arnold's fat kid, he hardly left his sofa, where he listened to the radio. He didn't even drive his mother to deliver her rolls to the greengrocer. Even Arnold wouldn't drive her.

Thinking about driving, he veered off. Deputy Parker needed his own transportation and Jack Summer wanted to sell his motorcycle so he could take Mrs. Towerton to dinner somewhere nice. He rang up Parker at his apartment over the greengrocer's shop.

"Are you in the middle of anything right now?" Howard asked.

"I'm just reading Mrs. Smithson's recipe book. You need me?"

"No, but you need to know something I'd forgotten to tell you. Jack Summer is looking for a used car and wants to sell his motorcycle. It even has a sidecar. I've already told Jack that a vehicle is beyond my budget. But maybe there's some way to work it out."

"How much does he want to be paid for it?"

"I didn't even ask," Howard replied. "You might go over to the newspaper office and see what he says. I shouldn't tell you this, but he's a bit anxious to get a real automobile. He also wants to interview you for the next issue of the *Voorburg Times*. He always wants to introduce newcomers to his readers."

"That's sort of embarrassing. As for the motorcycle, I'd love to buy it. I've got a little bit saved up. Maybe he'd let me make a down payment."

"You and Jack need to work this out yourselves."

As soon as the contracts were signed on Tuesday with the Harbinger boys and Mrs. Gasset, progress on the mail sorting station moved quickly. Robert was surprised that all the town council required was a normal business property tax to be paid on the basis of income. And it was only 1.5 percent of gross receipts. That was a lot less than Robert had expected them to ask from Mrs. Gasset. There had been conversations earlier about paying back the cost with half the proceeds of the sale of the boxes and annual fees. Mrs. Gasset would make a good deal more money than was being payed outright. *And so she should,* Robert thought. Of course, he'd help get everything done as soon as the boxes were completed. Each box needed to be numbered at the back end. Robert, who had fairly good handwriting, would volunteer to do that. And maybe he'd help her out a bit for the first few heavy Monday morning sortings. He was beginning to realize what a swell young woman she was. It would be a pleasure to spend a little free time with her.

Harry Harbinger had presented two different plans for the setup. The council let him decide which would be easier and most efficient. It was only a few hours after the council had made these decisions that Harry and Jim were at the train station taking detailed measurements. By the end of the day, the actual work had begun. Boxes were being created and glued together with additional nails to make sure they were sturdy.

Robert was, naturally, getting in their way, offering—fruitlessly—to be allowed to help. "I'll bet you don't even own your own hammer," Harry said.

"No, but I could buy my own," Robert claimed.

"Making this happen is enough," Harry said kindly. "We know what we're doing and don't need anybody's help."

Robert gave up. But he still sat in one of the chairs meant for people waiting for their trains to arrive. He wanted to at least observe.

At lunchtime, the Harbinger boys unpacked their sandwiches and Robert went to fetch Chief Walker. "You must see this. The boys are eating their lunch and we can go to Mabel's afterward."

Howard could hardly refuse. "After all, the mail sorting station is named for you, at my urging."

"Is it really going to be? I thought you were kidding. Wait until I tell Lily this. She'll be green with envy. Come on, Howard. I want you to see this before the Harbingers are through with their lunch."

Lily, somewhat to Robert's predictions, wasn't envious. Instead, she praised him for his concern and tenacity.

But later in the evening, Robert thought of a few other things that needed to be done. He called Mrs. Gasset and asked to meet her on one of her breaks to find out where he could locate duplicate numbered tickets for the lottery.

When he met her at the bench across the street, she already had the information and had written out an address on a small piece of paper. "It's one of my jobs to order new tickets for the box office when they start to run low. Here's the address in Poughkeepsie. If you could buy them before I give my boss my notice, I'd pay you back out of the proceeds of the lottery for the boxes."

"No need to do that," Robert said.

"You might not need the money, but I need to be fair."

Later that evening, Robert asked Lily, "Do we pay a business tax from what we earn from our boarders?"

"Of course we do. It's not much of a tax."

"I know. I learned that today. I have to go to Poughkeepsie to buy the lottery tickets. Want to ride along tomorrow?"

"That sounds nice. I've been cooped up inside too much with my reading lately. I've been alternating the mystery books you bought me for my birthday with the textbooks Dr. Toller lent me. I'll have to find a scarf though."

CHAPTER EIGHTEEN

Friday, May 12, through Monday, May 15

JACK SUMMER'S whole front page of the *Voorburg Times* was headed:

BOOKS!

Underneath this headline was a horrible picture he'd received via the press service he paid for. A night scene that showed a great blazing fire and armed men in brown SA uniforms either tossing books onto the file, or holding their guns trained on the crowds. Women were weeping, and children ran around as if it were a happy bonfire.

The text inside the front page explained that on the tenth of May German students who were enthralled by Hitler had burned thousands of books, mostly by Jewish intellectuals. Albert Einstein, Sigmund Freud, H. G.

Wells, Ernest Hemingway, Bertolt Brecht, even Helen Keller and Jack London. They especially went after Heinrich Heine, who had written more than a hundred years earlier, "When one burns books, one will soon burn people."

They also burned family Bibles, Talmuds, and anything not written in German. In the first fire in Berlin, overseen by Joseph Goebbels, propaganda minister for Hitler, more than thirty thousand books went up in flames.

Jack's editorial opinion was made clear in the next paragraph. "Should every good German have a copy of *Mein Kampf* on the bedside table and be required to memorize it?"

Mr. Kurtz picked up the paper and wept. He hadn't cried since he'd been eleven years old until that morning.

"The *criminals*! How dare they? Books are precious."

"Grandpa, I'm so sorry you saw this," his granddaughter said.

"Would you have hidden this horror from me? I hope you would not. Americans must know what they're up against. Hitler and his cronies are pure evil."

By Saturday, the thirteenth of May, the book-burning plague had also occurred in several large American cities.

Even Jack Summer couldn't figure out what was being burned and why. He called some of his reporter friends in other cities and asked who was doing the book burning, why, and what kinds of books.

The answers varied. Most of the other reporters had no idea, except to say, "They're young and stupid, and think it's all in good fun," almost all of them said in variations on the same theme.

"Most of the students I've talked to don't have any idea what or who started it, and they just went along with the idea," another reporter Jack spoke to said sadly. "It broke my spirit to see young people burning books."

And little Voorburg had its own book burning on Sunday in front of Mr. Kurtz's shop. This time on the sidewalk in front of his main window. Fortunately, a brief, heavy, and unexpected rain put the fire out a few moments later—before Chief Walker even reached town.

They were library books, all in German. Chief Walker handled them carefully, wearing gloves, and took them back to his office at the jail. On Monday he called several of the libraries they'd come from, asking if anyone remembered who had checked them out.

He collected three different names for the borrowers. But the descriptions, depending on the age of the librarian, were that it was a man in his sixties—this from seemingly young women from the sound of their voices. The older librarians who recalled him guessed late forties to mid-fifties. All agreed that he was lean, somewhat shorter than average, and had thinning brownish hair. One of them said he had brownish-red hair.

It was clear to Howard that the three names were all certain to be false. But the description, except for age, was likely to be the same person.

Chief Walker explained to all of them that books had been set afire and then doused by a short rain. He also told them the books might have been checked out by a suspect for former crimes and the books couldn't be returned until they were fingerprinted. This would take at least a week.

Walker thought that since Miss Exley hadn't been approached, but libraries both north and south of Voorburg, all close to Route 9, were chosen, this might be meaningful. Maybe because the man would be recognized as local? Or conversely, and more likely, that he didn't want to be seen in Voorburg by anyone.

Looking back later in the day, Walker realized that the books must have been set on fire at a little before two in the morning. Howard had awakened at the increasingly rare sound of rain at the open window of his bedroom at two. His phone had rung soon after Howard had closed the window, with a furious squawk from Mr. Kurtz the night of the second fire at his shop.

He called on Mrs. Smithson after he'd spoken to the libraries. "Mrs. Smithson, do you recall the man who came into your grandfather's shop the first day he was open for business?"

"Vaguely," she said. "I was still exhausted from the long trip. Why do you ask?"

"You said his first customer was Mrs. White wanting her girls' dresses let down, didn't you?"

"Yes. I do remember that."

"You also had a man come in?"

"Did I say that?"

"Robert said you did. What do you remember about him?"

"Nothing. He just came in while I was bringing a sandwich out front for my grandfather. He was so anxious to get everything in place that he hadn't even made himself breakfast."

"Do you recall what he looked like?"

"I had no reason to remember," Mrs. Smithson said. "All I saw was that he came in the door, and when Grandpa asked what he needed done, the man just shrugged. He didn't speak. He just stood there for a few minutes watching the pinking shears and scissors being hung on the wall and flat bundles of fabric being put on the shelves. When I came back to take away Grandpa's plate and glass of beer, nobody was in the shop."

"Was he tall or short? Fat or skinny? Bald or a redhead?"

"Chief Walker, I haven't any idea. I just thought he was rude and went back in the little kitchen to eat my own sandwich and make some coffee for Robert."

"I'm sorry to have bothered you with this. If you happen to think of anything else, let me know. I realize how awful these attacks on your grandfather are and am determined to find and lock up whoever is doing them."

Her reply was softer and stronger. "I know you do care almost as much as I do. I'm sorry to have been short with you."

"You're entitled to be," Howard replied. "I promise I won't let this go on without finding who is doing this to your grandfather."

Walker knew that he'd eventually find the man or woman, and now that he'd talked to the librarians, it seemed it clearly was a man. This man would go to jail for quite a while for two counts of attempted murder for trying to burn down the shop with the owner inside, and at least two counts of arson.

But he deeply regretted that he was still completely ignorant about the person who was responsible for the violent and vicious murder of Edwin McBride. Someone had to pay, perhaps with his own life, for that murder. Surely there would eventually be some clue to the perpetrator lurking in the back of his mind that would be blindingly obvious when his brain dislodged something trivial but important.

He dropped by the train station, hoping to get some answers from Harry or Jim. He was astonished at how well the Robert Brewster Letter and Package Center was coming along. All of the boxes were finished and Harry was working on the doors and the hardware for the combination locks.

"This is the hardest and most expensive part of the job," Harry said. "The rest is easy. Making a sorting table in back, and putting in a door with a lock, so nobody else can get in except for Mrs. Gasset."

"Where is Jim today?"

"He's on an emergency call. One of Mrs. Smithson's hot water systems has blown up. He's turned off the water and gone to Poughkeepsie to buy a new one. Excuse me, but could you move over a bit? I'm ready for the next bank of slots to get their doors."

Walker took a seat as close as he could get without being in Harry's way. He didn't want to be overheard by anyone else. "Harry, did Edwin ever have company? Did any of his old friends from his neighborhood come to visit him?"

"One tall blond man visited him. But it was weeks ago. Edwin told us he was an old friend from his childhood."

That confirmed what Deputy Parker had overheard.

"Oh, there was one other visitor. That tart in the red dress who used to hang around in the middle of town."

"Did she stay?"

Harry laughed. "No. Edwin was deeply embarrassed and told her to go away. He slammed the shed door in her face. I was working in the back of the house and saw and heard all of it. Then she came after me. I also told her to get lost. That I didn't need a disease. That really made her mad."

"Nobody else? You're sure?"

"No. How could I be sure? I'm seldom at home. Neither is Jim. We occasionally bring something home to work on, like Mrs. White's little chest, which she wanted painted red. But that's unusual." Harry went on, clearly annoyed by this conversation, which was interfering with his work. "If he'd had a friend visit, he probably wouldn't have even mentioned it. Besides, he spent most of his days at the train station. He'd sometimes buy a sandwich at Mabel's and take it home to eat between passenger trains."

"I'm sorry to have taken up your time," Walker said, a bit angry for no good reason. Except for pure frustration. He still had no idea who and why somebody would murder a nice, hardworking man.

CHAPTER NINETEEN

Tuesday, May 16, through Saturday, May 20

ROBERT WOKE UP ON TUESDAY with a brilliant idea. He'd have to call Mr. Winchel immediately. The tickets for the mail sorting center were to go on sale the next day and the drawing would be the next Saturday.

"Mr. Winchel, I want to rename the letter and package center. It should be the Edwin McBride Letter and Package Center."

"Why? You did all the work to get this set up. It should be named for you," Mr. Winchel said.

"But I started it first to keep the snoops from pawing through the mail, and then it became important to give poor Edwin a decent paying job so he'd be able to rent or buy a house or apartment. He deserves it more than I do."

"Do you really feel that strongly about this?" Winchel asked.

"I do."

"In that case it will be renamed. And I admire you for the idea."

The next thing Robert did was to dip into the money that was his share of what he had discovered in the first book in the library to buy tickets for himself, Lily, Mr. Prinney, Mrs. Prinney, Mimi the maid, Phoebe Twinkle, Mrs. Tarkington, both Harbinger boys, Chief Walker, Ron Parker, Jack Summer, Miss Exley, Mr. Kurtz, Mrs. Smithson, Mrs. Gasset, and Mrs. Towerton. He'd donate tickets to the town council members—except Arnold Wood, a man he hoped he'd never have to deal with again. He'd also go around to all the people who signed the petition to offer to sell them a ticket so they wouldn't have to wait in line to buy one. It would take him all day, but he owed it to them to get the first numbers.

The sorting center wasn't quite done yet, but it would be ready on the next Saturday, Harry had promised. Robert would also have to find a container for the duplicate tickets, which Mrs. Gasset could draw from. He himself would be on hand to write down the winning numbers for her and help label the boxes inside and outside. He assumed that not all two hundred of the boxes would sell immediately. He'd already turned over the names of the people who'd bought or been given tickets, along with the money and the ticket numbers.

Mrs. Prinney had helped him make and put up a banner on the front of the train station giving the cost, the sale date of tickets, and the drawing date.

Robert was really excited that this enormous project would soon be done and the work he'd put into it. He was also pleased that it had been renamed.

It had taken him all day to give out or sell the tickets and make records of them, and he went home exhausted, but feeling smug. He slept like a rock and woke a little after nine in the morning on Thursday. A quick shave and shower, two slices of toast, and he was off to the train station.

He was glad to see a fairly long line of people waiting to buy their tickets. Maybe thirty-five of them. He had trouble finding a parking place for the Duesie. When he found a spot near Mr. Prinney's office, he went inside the train station and asked Mrs. Gasset if she needed help. She claimed she was on top of it so far in keeping records. But she'd hoped he'd be around when the drawing of the tickets took place at ten o'clock Saturday. That, she suspected, was going to be a two-person job to keep track of who had won, and which box they'd chosen to use.

Harry and his brother Jim were almost done. All that was left was putting the last of the numbers on the boxes and fitting the lock on the back room.

Robert said, "I've turned over a significant amount of

money and tickets to Mrs. Gasset. Maybe you could do the lock before finishing the numbers. You still have two more full days to finish the box numbers."

"There's already money in there?"

"Yes, I paid for tickets for everybody at Grace and Favor and you two, and the town council," Robert admitted.

"You're crazy to do that," Jim said.

"No, I'm not. I wanted to. And money is money no matter who pays it."

Chief Howard Walker also woke up with a brilliant idea. But it was in the middle of the night. He thought it meant something important. He knew he should write it down, but he told himself firmly to remember it until morning.

By the next morning the idea had faded. He *really* should have at least made a note, a word or two on some scrap of paper. He thought it had to do with something that happened quite a long time ago. Something perhaps involving the swastika. Or not.

This had happened to him before. A good idea in a dream, then lost. But it always came back from wherever it was hidden in his brain. Sometimes quite suddenly when he was brooding over something else entirely. Usually it was trivial. The name of someone he once knew that suddenly came out his mouth when he'd given up on ever knowing.

But this vivid dream, now missing, was important. That he knew for sure.

On Saturday the twentieth of May the train station had a line of people outside waiting for mailboxes. Howard realized that he should be on hand. A lot of money was going to be taken in and The Law should be there to watch over it.

Somebody had lent Mrs. Gasset a long table to place in front of the boxes. She had two baskets ready. One for the cash. The other for information. She had a big pile of index cards. Each person whose number was drawn had to fill out his or her name, the number of the box chosen, and if they had a lock, put down the combination in case they forgot it.

As Howard arrived, at ten in the morning, the drawing had just commenced. The first number drawn went to a man Howard didn't recognize. He said, "Miss, there's no reason for you to know my combination. I won't forget it."

"Sir, it's *Mrs.* Gasset, and if you do forget and I don't know it, you will have to hire someone at your own expense to cut the lock off."

This convinced him to put down the combination.

Robert kept worrying over things he'd forgotten. The table in front, for example. It was Mrs. Gasset's duty to endorse every check with the whole name of the sorting center and drive somewhere to open a bank account.

Only about half the people had acquired a lock. The other half had to drive to a town that had a hardware store to buy one. Walker placed himself next to the basket with the cash, and Robert kept an eagle eye on the one with the names and the numbers of the boxes they'd selected. He was going to label them from inside the sorting area.

"What if I get a big package that won't fit in the box?" one of the buyers asked.

"You'd get a pink notice in the box notifying you to knock on the door, and I'd bring the package out. I won't be here in the evenings though."

"Whoever thought this out was smart," the woman said with a smile. "I'm so glad this was done."

It took four hours with one twenty-minute break for people who needed to use the station's bathroom or buy a candy bar or crackers from the vending machine. At intervals throughout, Robert announced loudly that the townspeople had Harry and Jim Harbinger to thank for building this fine sorting area. The drawing wasn't completed until nearly four o'clock. Howard, Robert, and Susan Gasset were all exhausted from simply standing around. One hundred and thirty-two boxes had been purchased.

When all the buyers were gone, the three of them allowed themselves a short break. Howard and Susan sat down while Robert ran over to Mabel's to buy sandwiches and drinks. He ate quickly, then went behind the boxes to start writing the people's names and box numbers and glueing them down under each box. He also took the basket with the money back where nobody else would know where it was.

Mrs. White appeared shortly and folded up the table she'd lent them. Howard carried it out to her big car to tie it on top with her rope. She'd brought along a bedspread to put under the table so it wouldn't hurt the paint on top of her car.

"I bought a box right in the middle. This was a wonderful idea. Who thought it up?"

"Robert Brewster. It was going to be named for him for all his efforts," Howard told her, "but at the last minute he decided it should be named after the man who needed the job of sorter."

"How generous of Mr. Brewster. I've always thought well of him and now I think even more what a fine young man he is."

A few minutes later, Robert poked his head out the door and said, "Mrs. Gasset, I forgot to get you a stamp to endorse the checks."

She smiled. "I already bought a stamp and two ink pads. Oh, and my sister Bernadette has volunteered to do the bookkeeping and fill out the tax forms. She's so grateful that I can be home in the evening to feed the children and put them to bed. She hates having to read them all stories before they go to sleep. I've already put a dollar into the bank in Cold Spring. Bernadette will also deposit the money."

Robert sighed with relief, and felt a bit guilty about secretly thinking badly of Bernadette.

Most of the last bags of mail on the floor had already been picked through by the people who had bought boxes. But Mrs. Gasset wanted to take the rest back and file the unclaimed mail in the right box if someone had purchased a box and forgotten to look through the mailbags that arrived earlier on Saturday.

"You've already had a very long day," Chief Walker said. "Just leave the bag in the back, lock up, and do it sometime tomorrow. There aren't deliveries on Sunday and you can get some rest."

"That's an excellent idea. I'll take you up on it. But first I need to shop for something to make for dinner. Something really good. Pork chops, stuffing, gravy, and mashed potatoes. And the carrots the kids won't eat, but Bernadette can give them to her rabbits later."

Chief Walker said, "I'll wait for you while you go to

the greengrocer and the butcher. You shouldn't be walking home with all that money and the checks. And I'll drive your sister to the bank."

"You don't intend to do this all the time, do you?"

"Only when it's a lot of money."

He waited for her outside the butcher's shop with the small locked steel box under the passenger seat until she'd done her shopping and drove her home.

CHAPTER TWENTY

AFTER HOWARD DROPPED OFF MRS. GASSET and headed back to Grace and Favor, a random thought came to his mind. It had to do with the color red, but wasn't what he'd dreamed about. The person, whom he now knew was a man, took the paint can back to Harry's work area behind their house. He didn't return the paintbrush. He'd probably just pitched the brush into someone else's trash.

The point was, why did he return the paint can?

He was obviously a sour, unpleasant person to keep harassing Mr. Kurtz. So why bring the paint can back to Harry and Jim's house? Did he have a weird streak of honor? It was okay to paint a swastika on the window of a man who had narrowly missed being arrested by the Nazis? Setting the fires wasn't just arson. It was two cases of attempted murder. But stealing a can of paint wasn't right. Or moral. What kind of bizarre personality was Howard dealing with and trying to find?

He'd never come across someone with such skewed motives. Except maybe Arnold Wood. But he was an exception. All his motives were simply selfish and mostly vulgar as well. And he only came to town for meetings of the town council. Otherwise, nobody ever saw him.

After dinner, Howard found Lily reading by the open window in the library.

"Answer a question for me, would you?"

She put her book aside and said, "Gladly."

"If you wanted to paint a red swastika on a person's window, wouldn't you go buy the paint and the brush in some town where nobody knew you? And why would you throw away the brush, much less bring the paint can back to where you found it?"

Lily smiled. "First, I'd never have reason to paint a swastika anywhere, but if I needed to, you're right. I'd buy the supplies with cash where nobody knew me. As for the brush, it was probably dried up and just buried in someone's trash. And I certainly would have sealed up the can and disposed of it as well."

"That's exactly what I'd have done in theory, too," Walker said. "So how did the swastika painter even find the paint in Harry's backyard, and why on earth return it?"

"Let me think on that for a while," Lily said, frowning. "There doesn't seem to be a logical reason for that. But the painter must have had some strange ideas."

Lily never knew the answer, nor did Howard until later.

On Monday, Walker drove Bernadette to the bank in Cold Spring. Monday was the heaviest mail day, and Mrs. Gasset couldn't get away. Thank goodness the children were still in school and he didn't have to fill the back of the police car with little kids. One was only in kindergarten, so they had to be back by noon and made it in plenty of time.

Bernadette was very pleasant. "It was so nice of Mr. Brewster to get my sister this job. She can be home in the evening with the children. And she'll make a lot more money than she did at the theater, selling tickets. The owner had the nerve to ask me to fill in for her. Can you imagine?"

"You'd probably be good at it, wouldn't you?" Howard asked. "You have good math skills, I understand from Mrs. Gasset."

"Yes, I do. But I wouldn't want the job. Having to be busy every night, like my sister was. I'm taking a course by mail for becoming an accountant."

"Good for you," Howard said. "Here we are at the bank. I'll wait in front."

"Oh, do come inside. I want the clerk to know I had a police escort."

As he opened the door of the bank for her, she turned and whispered, "Just don't draw your gun."

Howard laughed. He had had no warning that Bernadette had a sense of humor.

On the way back to Voorburg, Walker asked Bernadette, "Have you ever come across a man somewhere between forty-five and sixty, small stature, thinning reddish or brown hair?"

"Not that I remember. I seldom come to Voorburg except to ship off the rabbit furs when they're clean and dry. Why do you want to know?"

"That's how a bunch of librarians described the man who checked out the German books that were set on fire in front of Mr. Kurtz's shop."

"It's a shame that he's being singled out for all these awful things. I've never met him. I do my own sewing when I need to. But I've heard that he's a nice man."

When Walker had dropped Bernadette off at her home, he went to his office at the jail and took up his thinking position, leaning back in his chair, feet on the desk. The description the librarians had come up with could describe half a dozen different men. But not Arnold Wood, unfortunately.

And he was still puzzled over why the man took the paint can, neatly capped, back to Harry's work area in his backyard. Why didn't he just throw it away when he disposed of the paintbrush?

Arnold Wood was right this time. Howard had taken far too long to unravel these crimes against Mr. Kurtz, and hadn't even made any progress in the investigation regarding the murder of Edwin McBride.

He'd asked questions of everyone who might know anything about either of the crimes and come up empty-handed. The fingerprint expert even had a whole set of the man's prints in the case of Mr. Kurtz. The method with which Edwin was strangled had been identified, but Walker still didn't know where the wire had been purchased. Maybe he should travel up and down the Hudson visiting hardware stores to see if he could get a description of who could have bought the wire.

But what good would it do? Whoever bought it certainly hadn't given a name. And if he had bought it at a hardware store—and he could have bought it elsewhere—like a company that sold cheese or bread, nobody would remember after all this time what the person looked like. Or care.

He simply couldn't leave Edwin's death to be forever unsolved. There must have been some sort of clue in the elusive dream, which he was still unable to remember.

Deputy Parker came into the jail building and asked,

"Anything I can do? I'm feeling useless. I don't feel that I'm earning my salary."

"Not right now. I'm still trying to figure out McBride's murder. Where would you get a wire with small teeth like that? I've given it some thought. I don't think hardware stores would carry such a specialized kind of wire."

"Who would?"

"Jewelry stores, I assume, would know. And it could also be used for slicing bread or cheese."

Parker was impressed. "I'd never have thought of that."

"You would if you put your mind to it. Have you worked out something with Jack Summer about cars and motorcycles?"

"Almost. Jack's found a car he likes. And as soon as he buys it, he'll sell me the motorcycle. I get to pay on time payments. He's so anxious to get rid of it that he's given me a bargain price."

"I'm glad this is working out for both of you. You could earn your keep by finding a jewelry store somewhere near when you get the motorcycle. They'll know where a wire like that could be purchased."

"I should have the motorcycle by tomorrow. I'll go to the library and look in phone books today."

Howard grinned. "That's something I hadn't thought about. You *are* earning your keep."

Mrs. White had come back to Mr. Kurtz's shop to pick up her daughter's dresses and was enormously impressed with what a good job he did. She also brought along the dress that the other surly tailor had messed up.

Mr. Kurtz told her to go in the back room and change into the flawed dress and come back out. She did so. He almost lost his temper. "That's terrible. Completely wrong."

He took out his chalk and marked the shoulder lines, and said, "Even if the other man had done it right, the sleeves would have been too long. But I can fix everything. First, I have to carefully rip out what he did, then start over. Put your other clothing back on and I'll have it ready in three days."

"I'm so glad you can do this right. I know I can trust you. I'm tempted to go back and tell him how awful he is and how you undid his mistakes."

"It's up to you. But it would probably upset you more than him."

"You're probably right. My husband and I are going on a trip soon. Could you have the dress ready by Friday? We're driving to see my husband's new granddaughter in Albany."

"I could have it ready by Wednesday."

Ron Parker came back to the jail the next day. "I charged a phone call to your office. It was long distance. I'll pay you back if you want."

"You don't have to pay when you're doing your job."

"I'm not sure you're going to like what I found out."

"Tell me," Howard said, as the front legs of his chair went back down to the floor.

"I called a jewelry place and asked if they sold the kind of wire that could cut through a ring. They told me no. They order it in six-inch sections from time to time from a company in New York City."

"You called them, I suppose?"

"I did. I asked them if they'd had an order for a longer length of this kind of wire recently. They were surprised at the question and waffled a bit until I explained that I was the deputy to the chief of police of Voorburg-on-Hudson and was asking them in connection with a murder that involved using such a wire.

"Suddenly the guy on the phone went silent. I thought he'd hung up at first, but then he said, 'Murder? With a wire from us?' "

"Naturally he'd be wary. Companies don't like their products and murder in the same sentence. Go on—"

"That's what I figured. I assured him that they

wouldn't be held responsible, but might have to come to identify whether or not a certain person made the purchase at some time in the last few weeks."

"Could the person you were speaking to remember what he looked like?"

"This is the part you'll either love or hate."

Parker paused to take a deep breath and spit it out as fast as he could. "A man in his late forties or early fifties. Thinning, dirty brown hair. Short stature. Small hands. Shabby clothing."

CHAPTER TWENTY-ONE

HOWARD WALKER LEANED his elbows on the desk and stared at Deputy Parker for a long moment.

He finally said, "I'm stunned. I was sure we had two different cases and two criminals to pursue. You did good! So it's certainly the same man who the librarians described as stealing the books, who also bought the long section of wire to strangle McBride."

"You're relieved?" Ron asked.

"Relieved? Yes. Instead of trying to find two men to put away for life, we need to find the one right man."

"And how do we find him?"

"We just keep asking questions. I don't believe he's local. I know almost everyone who lives anywhere near Voorburg—at least by sight, if not by name. It's a shame I don't know one of those artists that newspapers use to make a face that can be identified by several people who have all seen the same person. Maybe Jack Summer could help us out."

"Before you ask Jack, let me try it. I drew all my classmates, all thirteen of them when we finished eighth grade. I was pretty good at it. The teachers and the kids themselves said I got them just right."

"Why didn't you tell me this before?"

"You never asked," Deputy Parker said.

"Then let's go buy you a bunch of paper, pencils, and erasers, and interview the librarians."

"I have paper and pencils already. In fact, I've made drawings of you, Jack Summer, and Mrs. Smithson. I'll go get them to show you."

Parker must have run to his apartment and back. He returned in minutes, out of breath.

Chief Walker thought they were excellent representations of all three. Though he himself looked a bit crankier than usual. That was because he'd been cranky most of the time Ron Parker had been his deputy.

On the other hand, Ron had seen all these people several times. The librarians had only seen the man he and Ron were looking for once, and briefly. It certainly wouldn't hurt to give it a try, however.

"I'll call the exchange and tell them we're out of town."

"Want to ride in the sidecar of the cycle? Jack got his automobile and turned it over to me this morning."

"Not on your life!" Howard said. "I wouldn't even fit into it. We'll take my car."

It took them all the rest of the day. The first two librarians who had seen the man who borrowed the German books disagreed with each other.

"His nose was thinner, and he was older."

"This picture the young man has drawn is about the right age," the second claimed. "But his face was more wrinkled. Lots of frown lines."

Parker erased and redid the picture. "Is that better?"

"Sort of," the first said.

"Only a little bit," the second replied.

"We're going to several other libraries. We may be back to you with other pictures."

Both were flattered.

At the next closest library, Deputy Parker found the only person who had seen the man. "I have a good memory for faces," she said. "This isn't quite right. His nose was pointy. His hair was thinner and looked greasy."

With more erasing, she almost agreed. "He scowled at us when we insisted that he sign up for a library card. His eyes were darker and the eyebrows skimpier."

On the third try, with Parker using a clean eraser, she said it was almost right. She studied it for a long time and asked, as if embarrassed, if the deputy could make him look a little meaner.

He said, "Meaner?"

"Eyes a little closer together."

When he moved the eyes a smidgen, she said, "That's *him*."

With thanks, they took off for one more library.

This librarian was outraged that they still didn't have their books back yet. The chief of police had promised they'd be returned when they'd been fingerprinted.

"Ma'am, you'll have them back tomorrow or the next day. I need to go fetch them. Only two have been finger-printed. The man who does it so well wants to make sure the same fingerprints are on each book. Does this picture look like the man who took your books?"

She considered long and hard. "It's very close. I think his chin was a little longer."

Parker's eraser and pencil worked this out.

"That's right," she said. "Now, make sure we get our books back!"

When they were in the police car, Ron said, "I must draw her. She's so unattractive that I want to save her."

"Save her?"

"Yes, commit her to eternal shame. She's quite re-markably hateful. Mrs. Smithson will love the picture. She once told me she'd had a teacher who was nice but the nastiest-looking woman in the world. I'll show her a nastier one who *isn't* nice."

They took the final picture back to the two librarians they'd first contacted.

"That's him!" one exclaimed.

"It's exactly right!" the other yelped.

When they arrived back in Voorburg, they stopped in at the jail office and Walker checked with the girl at the exchange. Nothing had happened in his absence. She sounded disappointed.

"Now we know what he looks like. What's next?" Deputy Parker asked.

"We try to get Jack Summer to place a copy of the drawing in the next issue of the *Voorburg Times*, simply saying, DO YOU KNOW THIS MAN?"

"Do you think anybody in Voorburg has seen him?" Parker asked. "He seems to always be here in the dead of night."

"Probably not. And Jack might not want to be involved. It might be too expensive for his budget to reproduce it. I'll talk to him about it."

Jack was wary about the cost of doing a clear reproduction of Deputy Parker's drawing. He called on Lily and Robert, who both happened to be home at Grace and

Favor. They owned the newspaper and almost never objected to what he printed in the *Voorburg Times*. This time it wasn't content, but expense.

"That's what the town pays Chief Walker to do," Lily said. "Protect us from criminals."

Robert chimed in, "I couldn't agree more. It's well worth the cost and I'm sure Mr. Prinney would agree."

"It will also take time. I can get it into the next issue of the paper on Friday the twenty-sixth. I'll also give Deputy Ron Parker credit for the drawing. This week's paper has a nice interview with him."

Walker hated to wait. It wasn't up to him to argue with the editor, especially when it was already too late to make a change.

Ron knew by now what his boss was thinking. "It can hold. It's already been a long time. We want to arrest him. He's probably going to get a death sentence. And when Jack publishes the picture somebody's bound to know who he is. That's what we need to keep in mind."

"You're talking to me as if you were my father," Walker said with a half laugh that didn't fool Ron.

"It's not that I'm telling you facts you don't already know. I'm just mentioning that we *will* get him."

"I hope we're both right about this. Let's go to Mabel's for lunch. It's meat loaf today. And it's on me this time."

They took Chief Walker's favorite table at the very back. They'd hardly sat down when Jim Harbinger said, "Can I join you? It's meat loaf day."

Walker realized that the single person he hadn't talked to about Edwin was Jim. They placed their orders and while they waited Howard asked, "Did Edwin have any other visitors besides the gal in the red dress?"

"Only two. An old friend he'd known when he was a kid. But that was a long time ago. The other man he saw wasn't really visiting Edwin. Edwin always got up just before dawn to hear and see the birds. He had binoculars. He told me he saw the guy putting back the can of red paint and yelled at him for being there."

"Why didn't Harry mention this when I asked him?" Walker asked.

"I don't think I mentioned it to him. Maybe Edwin didn't either."

"Did he describe the man?"

"Skinny, short, and thinning greasy hair."

"That's our man," Walker said to Parker.

"What man?" Jim asked.

"The one who came back and strangled Edwin."

"You're kidding, right?"

"I'm certain. After lunch go to Jack's office and take a look at the drawing Deputy Parker made of him. The drawing and your description match exactly."

The three orders of meat loaf, with mashed potatoes, gravy, and overcooked green beans arrived, and they all shoveled it down as if they hadn't eaten for days.

Jim finished first and asked, "How are you going to find the man who killed Edwin?"

"We're hoping when the picture appears in the next newspaper someone here will recognize him."

"How did Deputy Parker know what he looked like?"

Parker explained about the librarians who'd all seen him when he checked out the German books to set on fire at the tailor's.

"You draw good?"

"I hope I have," Parker replied.

CHAPTER TWENTY-TWO

Friday, May 26

THE PICTURE IN THE FRIDAY PAPER was well printed and clear. Walker expected a rash of callers to ring up and identify the man in the picture. A few did call.

"That looks a lot like a man I knew in Ohio."

"How long ago was that?"

"About twenty years ago. He was a farmer."

Walker had to thank him even though this man wouldn't have looked like the picture twenty years later.

Another caller said, "The picture looks like a man I saw when I was in California last week in a restaurant."

The man they were looking for had been in Voorburg last week burning trash and books. And he didn't look like he had the money to fly to and back from California.

"Give me your number and I'll get in touch if you're right," Walker said.

And that was the end of the calls that day. Walker tried to put a good interpretation on this. Not everybody read the paper as soon as it was delivered. Many saved it to read over the weekend.

Maybe this wasn't going to work at all. Few people outside Voorburg and its surrounding farms even got a copy. Walker was fairly sure this wasn't somebody who lived anywhere near Voorburg.

Again on Saturday and Sunday there were a few calls. All entirely unlikely. The callers said (as the first one had) they knew a man who looked like the picture in the *Voorburg Times* ten or fifteen years ago in Oregon. Or Kansas. Or Nevada.

It wasn't until the next Monday morning that he heard from Mrs. White. "Chief Walker, Henry and I have been out of town and I only read the Friday edition of the *Voorburg Times* today. I know who he is."

"Are you sure?" Howard thought this was another of those useless calls.

"Absolutely. It's the tailor in Cold Spring who wrecked my new dress."

Walker leaned forward and asked a bit too loudly, "Do you know his name?"

"Not exactly. The shop is halfway down the hill on the north side of town and called simply 'Tailoring.' I paid in cash and never knew his name. But I assume you already know this."

"No, I had a lot of calls but none of them were any good."

"You're going to arrest him, I assume. The paper didn't say why he was being sought but that's the usual reason for a newspaper to print a picture just saying, DO YOU KNOW THIS MAN?"

"That's right. He's responsible for one murder and two attempts at murder as well as two counts of arson. Thank you so much for letting me know."

"Are you arresting him today?" she asked. "I hope so. Such a dangerous man. I'd never have guessed. I just knew he was nasty and incompetent. I told Mr. Kurtz I was going to take the dress back to the other tailor to show him how it should have been fixed. Thank goodness I didn't do that. He might have murdered me next." She laughed, but it was a feeble, half-scared noise.

"I have to get his fingerprints before we arrest him. I want to be a hundred percent positive that I have the right man. Thanks again, Mrs. White."

He called Parker. "I think we've got our man. But we need fingerprints. And that takes a warrant. I don't have enough proof to get a warrant. Just the word of someone else."

"Coffee cup," Parker said. "It worked before."

"But what if he recognizes me?" Howard asked. "At one time or another I've been in most of the towns around here in uniform. In fact, I was in uniform when I took Bernadette to the bank in Cold Spring, and that was only a few days ago."

"I've never been in Cold Spring at all," Parker said.

"I think you're a bit too young to pull off the coffee cup thing. I think it needs to be done by someone older and obviously harmless. Preferably white-haired. We can't afford to botch this."

Parker asked, "Does Mrs. White have a husband? Is he old enough?"

"Yes. He's her second husband. Her first one was killed." He didn't want to share any more information about her first husband's death.

"I think I might talk to him. I owe it to Mrs. White," Howard said. "She's the one who knew him. I'll give her husband a call. I'll ask him to come into the office."

Henry White was well aware of his moral debt to Chief Walker and said he'd be glad to help. "I can do the dotty old guy as well as anybody else. Tell me what you want me to do."

"We need his fingerprints."

"How can I get them?" Henry asked.

"The coffee cup ploy," Howard said with a smile. "I'll buy a very smooth coffee cup, wash it off thoroughly, and only touch the handle to put it in a paper bag. You take it along to Cold Spring. Park where the car you drive can't be seen."

Henry was grinning. "What next?"

"You go into the tailor's shop. It's halfway down the steep main street on the left. By the way, you didn't go into the shop when your wife took her dress to be fixed, did you?"

"No. She drove herself. But it's our only car. Maybe I should borrow someone else's."

"Jack has a new car," Parker put in. "Not really new. Just new to him. If he doesn't want to lend his, I'm sure Mrs. Smithson would provide hers to Mr. White."

"Smart deputy you've got," Henry White said.

"I think Jack's would be better," Howard said. "Mrs. Smithson inherited a lot of rental property from her late husband. Some of the buildings might be in Cold Spring. If we promise Jack the whole story for his paper as soon as we arrest this man, he'll be glad to lend you his car.

"You do this," Walker went on. "Park where the tailor in Cold Spring can't see the car, take the cup out of the bag by the handle. Don't touch the rest of it. Walk in, act frantic. Say your wife is in the car and you think she's ill. She needs a big cup of water to take her medicine. Shove the cup into his hands before he can grasp the handle. Thank him profusely and hurry outside, holding the cup by the handle again. Pour out the water when you get back to the car and put it back in the paper bag. Bring it to me and I'll take it to the fingerprint expert in Newburg. He already has all the fingerprints of the perp from a trash can. It won't take long to verify them."

"I'll be delighted to help this way. And my wife will be proud of me for getting even with him for messing up that dress. She was really angry about that."

Henry set out to borrow Jack's car. He was happy to oblige when he knew the reason why Mr. White needed it. Henry went home, told his wife what he was doing, and put on his old patched dungarees and an old plaid shirt with one elbow out. These were his gardening clothes.

He drove to Cold Spring with the cup in its paper bag and parked around the corner a block away from the tailor's shop. He went around the corner, holding the cup by its handle, and rushed into the shop. "My wife's horribly sick. She forgot to take her medicine this morning. Could you fill this cup with water for me?"

He'd said this so hysterically and looked so badly dressed that the tailor grabbed the cup, filled it, and watched with relief as Henry called "Thanks!" over his shoulder and fled back up the street. He'd tipped out the water as soon as he was out of sight from the shop for fear the water would slop out and wash away the fingerprints. He didn't know much about such things. He drove hell for leather, grinning, back to the Voorburg jail and handed over the paper bag.

"That was sort of fun," he admitted.

Walker looked over the way he was dressed and laughed. "You sure put on a trashy set of clothes."

"I'd have spoken as if I were from West Virginia if I had the accent down right. I've got to get Jack's car back to him and get home to tell Edith all about it."

CHAPTER TWENTY-THREE

Monday, May 29

"I DON'T WANT TO WAIT in case this man happens to see a copy of the *Voorburg Times*. It's unlikely. But I don't want to let him do a bolt," Howard Walker said to Deputy Parker. "We need backup though. He's likely to be violent. I'm going to call Chief Colling and see if he can give me two extra people. He has a much larger staff than I do. I'm glad I hand-delivered that cup and waited for the results."

The call was made, an explanation followed, and Colling agreed to send two of his biggest, strongest deputies. "I can have them there by noon with their own cars. I've been following this case in your local newspaper."

The other two deputies from Chief Colling's office arrived promptly at noon. Walker gave them a brief account of why he thought he needed them. "He's a violent and hateful person. Though he's small, he's mean and overcame a man substantially taller and stronger than himself and strangled him with a piece of wire that has tiny teeth that's meant to saw rings off fingers. All because the victim saw him return a can of paint he'd stolen."

All he heard at first was a disgusted sigh from both of them.

Walker said, "Deputy Parker and I will lead and you follow us to Cold Spring. Finding places to park on the main road is going to be difficult for three cars. So we'll wait up the street somewhere and all go in at the same time."

Everybody followed the directions, and they all walked into the tailor's shop together. The tailor merely looked at them complacently. Walker was astonished at how much he looked like Deputy Parker's drawing.

It was a shabby, dark front room with a long counter with spaces at the sides, and a few dusty tools scattered around on it. A shelf behind held disorderly bundles of ugly fabrics. Everything was dusty and smelled of cheap hair oil.

"Sir, what is your name?" Howard asked.

"What's it to you?" he said.

"We're here to arrest you. We'd like to have a name to attach to the paperwork."

"Homer Wilson."

It wasn't the name used on any of the library check-outs and might or might not be true. Walker really didn't care what the man's name was. Just that they got him charged and jailed.

Walker walked around the right side of the counter with handcuffs in his left hand. Suddenly the tailor lunged forward with open scissors in his hand and stabbed Walker in his upper arm. Walker quickly backed away, looking down at the blood gushing over his hand and the handcuffs. Ron Parker grabbed Walker's right arm. Walker had turned pale and was about to fall over, staggering to find something to hold on to to keep himself upright.

The other men ran around the left end of the counter, knocked the man to the floor, and there were gargling yelps of pain from painful kicks.

Parker heaved the bloody handcuffs over the counter and said, "One of you use these and hold him down, the other call an ambulance."

Then he stripped off Walker's jacket and shirt and lowered him carefully to the floor. Ripping apart a piece of his shirt he wrapped it tightly around Walker's left arm above the gaping, gushing bloody hole. Walker had turned even paler, his mouth a grimace of pain before he fainted.

"Give me something to twist this tighter," Ron said.

One of the officers, with all his weight holding down the tailor with his feet, rummaged around on the table and found a wooden mallet, while the other one was yelling at the tailor and giving him another kick. "Don't you dare try to get up, you murderer."

Ron said to them, "Take that man to Matteawan after the ambulance comes to take my boss to the hospital in Poughkeepsie. I'm going with him. I only have two jail cells and can't deal with him. The State Hospital for the Criminally Insane can handle him."

Parker checked Walker's pulse in his bloody left wrist. As far as Parker could gauge, it was a bit slow, but not dangerously so.

The sound of the ambulance wailing got louder and louder and a crowd had formed on the opposite side of the street as the tailor was dragged out, kicking and screaming obscenities.

Two men stopped in the middle of the road and ran inside with a gurney.

"Treat him gently. He's lost a lot of blood," Ron said, his voice firm.

"We can see that," one of them said softly.

"I'm coming with you."

"There's no need, and no room for you."

"He's my boss. He's a good man. I'm coming with you."

He didn't even notice that some part of the crowd had started seeping across the street behind the ambulance, trying to look in the back door and then moving furtively closer to the shop to see what had happened. A local officer had turned up to keep the snoops out of the shop. Parker grabbed Walker's uniform jacket, then ran into the street and climbed into the ambulance.

There was only a corner where Parker could cram himself into as the ambulance backed into a parking lot, turned around, and screamed off at a terrific speed up the steep main road.

"You did a good job with this tourniquet," the attendant shouted over the noise of the siren. "But it needs to be loosened occasionally."

"I knew that," Ron said. "I took a Red Cross First Aid course at the police college."

It seemed to take forever to get to Poughkeepsie even though they were going almost dangerously fast on Route 9. All Ron could do was to take Howard's shoes off and massage his feet, hoping it might bring him around. Finally he felt a toe move slightly.

"He's coming around slowly," the attendant yelled. Ron thought the attendant sounded as if he was smiling.

They suddenly took a turn so sharp that Ron bumped his shoulder hard against the framework of the vehicle.

With a subsequent slowing and stopping, the siren

died and the back door was jerked open. Two other men in white were waiting. They pulled out the gurney and locked the collapsing structure with the wheels in place. Ron stayed where he was until the process was completed and the men started running through the open doors of the hospital. Then Ron jumped out the back, clutching Walker's uniform jacket and his shoes, and ran after them.

A police officer guarding the door grabbed Ron's arm. "You can't go with him."

"I must!"

"They'll let you sit outside while they're working on him, if you behave. Is he a cop, too?"

"He's Howard Walker, the chief of police of Voorburg. My boss."

"I know him," the man said. "A good man."

Releasing his grip slightly, he added, "Come along. I'll show you where you can wash up. There's blood all over your hands and you'll scare patients and their visitors. Then I'll show you where you can sit and wait. I'll get a message through to the surgery room and tell them who he is, and to treat him well and that you're waiting to know how he is. Do you need me to sit with you? I could call somebody else to guard the emergency entrance."

"No. I'll be fine after I clean up. But please try to make somebody come tell me how he's doing."

"For Walker's sake, I'll do that."

Deputy Parker, sitting with Walker's shoes and jacket on the chair beside him, waited a full two hours and fifteen minutes before a middle-aged man with a bloody face mask pulled back over the top of his head sat down on the other side of Parker and turned toward him.

"You're Walker's deputy, aren't you?"

"I am. Is he alive?"

"He is. By the way, I'm Dr. McCoy and I did the surgery. Chief Walker has a good chance of recovering completely if an infection doesn't set in. And I'm told that a piece of his shirt and the mallet are your work."

"They were," Ron said and told him about the Red Cross lessons. "Would you explain what you did in there?" Parker asked, gesturing toward the room where the surgery had taken place.

Dr. McCoy said, "It's like this—there is an artery that goes down the outside of your arm. For a short while, it's fairly close to the surface, then it ducks under muscles and goes down the rest of your arm. It isn't the main artery, but you need both. His attacker only cut halfway through it. If he'd cut clear through it, we couldn't have found both ends of it and your boss would have had to have half of his arm amputated, even if he didn't exsanguinate."

"What does that word mean?"

"Bleed to death before he got here. Oh dear, put your head down between your knees. I don't want you fainting on me," Dr. McCoy said.

Ron did so for a few minutes, then sat back up. "Sorry. I shouldn't have asked."

"You're entitled to ask. You're the hero here. We put him out, pulled back the skin and fat, let it bleed out a little to wash out any germs. Then we put our own tourniquet back on, to stop the blood flow. Blotted the blood all out, sewed up the cut in the artery with lots of little stitches, shook sulfa into the wound, sewed back the skin, and put gauze around it."

"When can I see him?"

"Not until tomorrow at least. He won't completely awaken until morning. Go home and get some rest."

"I have no way to go home. I came in the ambulance."

"In that case, I'll write up an order to give you a room here tonight and a chit for the hospital cafeteria. It's not very good, but it's healthy. I'll have a nurse show you to a room. There's a shower room on each wing with towels, soap, and robes. I'll walk you to the desk to find a nurse if you're ready."

"I'm fine now."

CHAPTER TWENTY-FOUR

WHEN THEY GOT TO THE NURSING STATION, Dr. McCoy introduced Deputy Ron Parker to the head nurse. "He's a hero. He saved Chief of Police Howard Walker's life."

"No, I didn't. God and you did, Dr. McCoy."

"Don't be so modest."

"Deputy Parker," the nurse said. "I've had four calls for you from a Jack Summer, desperately asking to speak to you as soon as I could find you."

She looked around furtively for a moment. "You can call him from back here if you make it a very short call."

"I will."

He asked for the Voorburg exchange and was answered by one of the operators who never listened in. "Connect me to Jack Summer, please," he said.

Jack picked up on the first ring. "Ron! I've heard from

Colling's officers that Howard Walker's been stabbed and you're with him. Is he alive?"

"Yes, and likely to recover. I'm trapped here. Could you drive down around noon tomorrow? Someone has to be at the jail office while I'm gone."

"That's already taken care of," Jack replied. "One of Colling's men who was there is here now. I'll run over to the jail to tell him Walker's alive. He'll be relieved to hear it."

Ron said, "I have to hang up fast. I'm long distance against the rules. Be here at noon. Maybe we can both see him. And I can explain a lot more."

He hung up quickly and the nurse thanked him for being so fast. "I'll claim I had to make that call when the bill comes."

Dr. McCoy said, "Nurse Hawkin, brave Deputy Parker has no way to get back to Voorburg today, and he's exhausted. I'm authorizing a room with a private bath for him and a free dinner and breakfast here."

"The room will be a good one. I have two of the private ones available. But the food here is awful," Nurse Hawkin said.

"But nourishing," Dr. McCoy reminded her. Then he said to Parker, "Get a good long hot shower and even a nap if you can manage it. I'll eat here with you at six if you think of more questions you want to ask. Now follow Nurse Hawkin."

Ron did as he was told. Nurse Hawkin wanted to show him both available rooms, but Parker said she should choose. Either one would be fine with him.

She complimented him on being such a good young man and said to ring down to her if he needed anything. "I could find you some magazines to read if you want."

"I couldn't read anything right now. I just need to get clean and into a bed to think about today."

She shook his hand and went away, closing the door behind herself.

Parker threw off all his clothes and took the long hot shower the doctor had prescribed. He dried off, put on the robe that was hanging on the back of the bathroom door, and tested out the bed. It was nice and hard the way he liked beds. And had nice soft sheets. He'd always been told that hospital sheets were starched into boards you had to make bend.

The shower had eased the ache in his shoulder, and in spite of himself he fell fast asleep for almost two hours.

He hated getting dressed in his slightly bloodstained uniform, but there was nothing he could do about it. At least the uniform was dark blue and the dry blood hardly showed. He did call Nurse Hawkin and asked if he could have a toothbrush and a clothing brush if he came down to her desk.

"I'll have them sent up to you. You need to rest all you can."

Moments later a cute young nurse knocked on his door. "Nurse Hawkin said you needed these. But that she could do a better job than any man at getting blood out of clothing if you want to send yours down. They'll be back in an hour. Please let me take your jacket and trousers to her. Your shirt, too, if you need it cleaned."

"I probably do. I got blood all over myself."

He gathered up his pile of outwear and bundled it up for her. No reason to send his underwear along with such a pretty young girl. He'd be able to change it tomorrow when he got home.

True to her promise, she was back in an hour with the uniform jacket, trousers, and shirt on hangers, smelling fresh and still warm from an iron. He thanked her and hung them in the closet.

"Are you married, Deputy Parker, if you don't mind my asking?"

"No, I'm not," he said, fearing that he was blushing slightly.

"Neither am I." And with that she smiled and slipped out of the room, rattling slightly in her starchy nurse clothing.

Deputy Parker met Dr. McCoy at the door of the hospital cafeteria at six, as planned.

"How's my boss doing?"

"Very well. He's still not fully awake but his blood pressure is good, his temperature is normal. We're still giving him some drugs for the pain. But I think it's likely he'll come through fine. Let's go through the line and you can ask the rest of your questions while we eat."

Parker chose macaroni and cheese, two slices of meat loaf, green beans, and a roll. The macaroni was undercooked and tasteless. The meat loaf was overcooked and also tasteless. The green beans were old and tough. The roll was delicious.

"Sorry I suggested this," Dr. McCoy said. "We should have gone to the restaurant across the street. It's slightly better." Both of them pushed their plates away and Dr. McCoy said, "Have you thought of more questions?"

"A few. How long will you have to keep Chief Walker here?"

"At least five days. We need to watch carefully for infection. And I'll tell you a few other things. The inside stitches in the artery will be there forever. They may be uncomfortable as they stiffen up. He might want to come back in a year or so and we'll lightly sedate him and remove them when the artery is thoroughly sealed up. It will be up to him."

"You'll explain all this to him before he leaves?"

"Of course. The arm is going to be sore for a while. He might want to keep it in a sling so he doesn't accidentally use it too much."

"Is the circulation in the rest of the arm okay?"

"Amazingly so. No bruising in the hand. He's a durable man. Do you happen to know his age?"

"No. I've only been his deputy for a short time, but I met him earlier when I worked for another chief of police. I'd guess a little over thirty."

"I'll be able to ask him when he comes around," Dr. McCoy said. "But that would be my guess, too."

"Will the town reporter who's coming to fetch me tomorrow be able to talk to him?"

"I don't know why not. It's up to the patient, not me. He'll be sitting up by morning. It's not good for his circulation to be horizontal for long periods. Anything else you want to ask?"

"Will he remember any of what happened to him?"

"Probably not."

"Should I tell him?"

"Not unless he asks," Dr. McCoy said. "I have to go back to work. I suggest you have your breakfast across the street. They do a really good ham and eggs and cinnamon toast."

They left the cafeteria and Dr. McCoy went back to work. Parker decided to go for a walk. He'd never been in

Poughkeepsie before. He'd ask the nurse at the desk what there was to see within walking distance.

She gave him a couple of brochures and a map. "We keep these for out-of-towners like you who are here to visit family members who are patients."

There didn't seem to be much close to the hospital. No museums. A couple of hotels, and a big park a mile away. He headed for the park and watched children feeding the ducks for a while. Then he followed some paths through pretty gardens. He knew nothing about flowers except that they looked pretty this time of year. Especially the many bushes that were blooming.

Bored, and aware that it would be dark in an hour or two, he strolled back to the hospital and sat on a bench outside for a while. Later, he'd go across the street and see if the restaurant Dr. McCoy told him about had good desserts.

But he couldn't take his mind away from the events of the earlier part of the day. It was the worst day of his life, seeing Walker faint, and seeing all that blood running over the dirty floor.

The next day, Parker was up early. He checked with Nurse Hawkin. "Dr. McCoy is doing another surgery right now," she said. "But he checked on your boss earlier and he's doing fine. Don't you worry."

Parker went to breakfast across the street and walked

around a bit more in the other direction. When he returned, Jack Summer was already waiting for him. "Are we allowed to see Howard today?"

"Yes, close to noon. It's up to him if he wants to see either of us."

"One of Colling's guys who went with you said you saved his life."

"I helped to. But it was the doctor who really saved him." Parker went on to repeat what Dr. McCoy had told him about the artery that was nicked. And the possibility of losing his arm if it had been cut clear through.

"But he says Walker is extremely durable and barring an infection he'll survive."

They waited near Nurse Hawkin's station. "That's a good nurse," Parker told Jack. "She even cleaned the blood off my uniform and had it pressed. I need to send her some nice flowers when I get back home. Does everybody in Voorburg know about this?"

"A lot of them asked me where you two had gone. I reported first to the people at Grace and Favor, of course. Robert was determined to come along and take Walker home in the Duesie right away," he added with a laugh. "I also told the greengrocer why you wouldn't be in your apartment until today. Oh, and Mrs. Gasset got wind of it and came in on one of her breaks to ask about what happened. I told her, truthfully, that I had no idea except that

Walker had been stabbed and was still alive. You're going to have to fill me in more on the way back to Voorburg."

"The doctor also told me something else you should know," Parker said. "We're not to tell Walker anything unless he asks."

CHAPTER TWENTY-FIVE

Tuesday, May 30

AT EXACTLY NOON, as Dr. McCoy had promised, he came out of Howard's hospital room and found Deputy Parker and Jack Summer waiting on a bench near the door. Both leaped to their feet.

"I'm Jack Summer, the editor of the *Voorburg Times*," Jack said, shaking the doctor's hand.

"Your chief of police is eager to see both of you. Go on in. Don't stay for more than twenty minutes. You are his first visitors and he'll tire easily. He's lost a lot of blood and needs a lot of sleep before it builds back up."

He opened the door for them and went away.

Howard Walker was sitting up in the bed. Parker almost got teary at how much better he looked. Howard was smiling. His face wasn't quite as pale as it was yesterday, and his left arm was in a lightweight sling.

"Am I ever glad to see you two. Pull up some chairs and talk to me. I don't remember anything after walking in the door of the tailor shop in Cold Spring."

He was looking at Deputy Parker, and went on to say, "They tell me you saved my life."

"I helped. But God and Dr. McCoy did the rest."

Howard put out his right hand to shake Parker's. "Do sit down, both of you. Where is the tailor we went to arrest?"

"At the Hospital for the Criminally Insane in Matteawan," Parker said. "I had him sent there because I couldn't get back to Voorburg. I'd ridden here in the ambulance with you."

"I'm surprised they let you do that."

Parker grinned. "They didn't let me. I forced myself in and sat in a corner near your feet."

Walker was silent for a moment then asked, "What did you do while we came here?"

Parker almost blushed. "I took off your shoes and massaged your feet. It was a dumb thing."

"I thought I'd dreamed that someone was messing around with my feet and I wondered why they were doing it. It really happened?"

"I just wanted to do something—anything for you," Parker admitted.

Walker closed his eyes for a few minutes, then opened

them and asked, "Who's taking care of Voorburg in our place?"

"One of Colling's men who was with us at the tailor shop."

"Who else knows about this?" Walker asked.

Jack said, "I was told by Colling's man that you'd been stabbed and taken away to the hospital in Poughkeepsie. That's all that I knew. I spent a lot of yesterday trying to get Parker on the phone at the hospital. Naturally nobody would tell me anything about any patient. Deputy Parker finally called back and said the surgery was over and you were alive."

"Then what?"

"I went up to Grace and Favor and told them where both of you were and that you'd been stabbed while arresting the man who killed Edwin McBride, and that you were alive but still unconscious after a successful operation. I also told the greengrocer why his upstairs tenant was missing. Then it got around to almost everybody. You'll be inundated by flowers and get-well cards by tomorrow."

He went on. "I'll bet Mrs. Prinney is making pots and pots of soup to force down you when you get back. I'm in the way right now. I'll leave you two to talk a little more. Deputy Parker, I'll wait for you in the parking lot to take you back to Voorburg."

Jack closed the door as he left.

"I want to go home," Walker said quietly with his eyes closed.

"In good time," Parker said. "I'll tell you the rest of it when and if you want to know. Get some more rest."

Parker wanted to touch him again, just out of respect, and he put his hand briefly on Howard's right hand before leaving. He stopped at the front desk to thank Nurse Hawkin again. "And there's something else. I have Chief Walker's uniform jacket and his shoes, but I need his trousers as well. Does anybody know what became of them?"

"I'll find out." She summoned the pretty nurse and said, "Please go find Chief Walker's trousers."

She was back in ten minutes with them in a big bag. "This will hold his jacket and shoes as well."

As Jack turned the car toward Voorburg, Parker told Jack almost everything the doctor had told him. All except the mention of bleeding to death.

When he got back to Voorburg, Parker asked the temporary substitute deputy to stay on for a little while. He took his motorcycle to the Hospital for the Criminally Insane where the tailor was locked up and asked permission to see him.

The tailor swore at him and tried, without success, to spit at him, but Parker ignored it and said, "I just have one question I hope you'll answer. The man you stabbed deserves to know. Why did you put the can of paint back where you found it?" It wouldn't hurt to make this man suppose his victim was dead.

The man, whoever he was, grinned. His teeth were greenish and chipped. As a child Parker had been taught that there is a God and there is a Devil, and he had now seen the Devil.

"You don't get it, do you?" the man said.

"No, I don't. But I'll pray that in heaven He'll know."

The man finally said, "You stupid kid. I wanted the police to think those dumb boys had painted the swastika."

Parker turned away and went back to Voorburg thinking, *Just wait until I tell Walker.*

The first thing Parker did when he again returned to Voorburg was to take Chief Walker's trousers and jacket to Mr. Kurtz to clean and fix the hole in the sleeve. "I'll do it gladly. No charge. He's a good man."

Parker then took Walker's shoes to the cobblers'. They were happy to clean up, shine, and resole them at no cost. His third call was on Jack Summer, telling him about the tailor and the cobbler and suggesting that if Jack wanted to, he could find a good white shirt for Walker. Jack agreed. "I'll pay Mr. Kurtz to make one. Since he has Walker's jacket, he'll make it the right size."

Ron was pleased. He knew that his boss would be humiliated to arrive at Grace and Favor in a hospital robe and slippers. He deserved to return to Voorburg with all the dignity that was due him.

Both Jack and Ron wanted to go back to Poughkeepsie the next day, just to check on how Walker was doing. Jack drove.

"Remind me to stop at a really good candy shop before we go to the hospital. I want to take a big box of chocolates to Nurse Hawkin."

As they drove, Jack asked Parker if he knew why the man who'd stabbed Walker had gone so far to scare, or possibly burn up his shop.

"I've given that a lot of thought," Parker said. "I've been in both of those tailor shops and Kurtz's is full of good German equipment. Scissors, shears, needles, a good sewing machine, and lots of nice European-made fabrics."

He went on, "I was only in the Cold Spring tailor's shop for a short time and it was dirty and grim. The tools on the counter were rusty. The only thing sharp he owned was the scissors he used to stab Chief Walker. I think he also hated Germans. Plain old jealousy and fear that he'd lose all his customers to Kurtz. I should have asked him when I spoke to him, but I was so revolted I just wanted to get away from him as soon as I could."

Jack nodded. "That sounds very likely."

As they were almost in Poughkeepsie, Parker said, "Keep your eye out for a candy store."

Here's a glimpse at the next
Jane Jeffry mystery

The Accidental Florist

by

Jill Churchill

Coming soon in hardcover
from William Morrow

Jane said, "No, I'm not angry. Before I asked you about the ring, I gave a lot of thought to a wedding. Here is how it's going to go. First, it happens when my parents can be there. They're in Denmark right now. Dad's translating for some Americans who want a contract to do something about drainage in Denmark.

Second, when my parents come, we'll have the 'real' wedding in front of the judge with just family. Shelley, as my Matron of Honor, my kids, I probably have to invite my mother-in-law, Thelma, and whoever you want as Best Man."

Mel, looking pole-axed, said, "I think that should be your uncle Jim. I've always admired him."

"Good. That's who I would have suggested. He thinks the world of both of us. Now, to the other rules. Your mother may come as well, if she wishes."

"I can't be sure of this part," Mel said.

"I wouldn't complain if she came. The third set of rules are this: Your mother can foot the bill for the second wedding. She can choose the food. She can choose the wine and invite mobs of their professional friends.

"The things she cannot do is choose my flowers or even suggest what I wear. She can't add bridesmaids or groomsmen."

"She's not going to like this, Janey."

"'Frankly, my dear, I don't give a damn,' to quote Rhett Butler. It's our fake wedding. And the bride and her parents make the decisions. I know they would agree with me since your mother has demanded to run the whole thing. You have to stand up to your mother on this or there's only the one wedding at the judge's chambers." Mel put his hands over his ears, and suddenly started laughing.

"Whatever you say. I wish you could be around when I tell her this. But you can't be. Because she's going to be very nasty about it. Will you do me a favor in return?"

"Probably. What is it?"

"Wear that gorgeous emerald colored suit Shelley made you buy. You look beautiful in that. And I want your Uncle Jim to be best man for both weddings."

"That's do-able. You really are my heart's desire." She started to tear up and Mel put his arms around her and kissed her forehead.

Jane's father couldn't get out of his translating duties to the Danes until the end of July, but her mother could come. Jane found this unacceptable. She didn't care when the wedding took place and Mel didn't either. So they'd wait till both of her parents could be there.

In the meantime, Jane started making lists. What closets would need to be purged? At least two.

How many more towels would she need when she was married. "Go for it," she said out loud. "Buy all new ones. Blue for him. Pink for me."

Another thing was getting the other half of the garage cleaned out.

She'd gone to look over it and there wasn't a thing in the other half that was worth more than a couple of bucks. Old table cloths that had mildewed, the lawn mower, a leaf blower, a snow blower, even a lot of the kids' old, dirty, disintegrating toys. If Todd wanted that half-a-million Legos he'd have to find a different place to store them or give them away to somebody younger.

Meanwhile, she'd go pick out an attractive shed to put at the side of the house to keep all those tools in. She'd go to Sears and make them bring one out and put it together. Then she'd hire some local teenaged boys from the neighborhood to move everything into it. In fact, Shelley's son

John would probably be glad to do it for the right amount of money. She'd ask Shelley about this.

And what about the beat-up desk and disgraceful but-sprung chair he loved to use when he was working at home? Where would that go? Todd's room? He'd moved his desk and bed into Mike's bedroom. Mike might want it back someday.

What about extending the house at the back behind the dining room? She could afford it. Thanks to her dead ex-husband's will, she had a perpetual third interest in the Jeffry family pharmacy because she'd contributed a substantial sum she'd inherited from a great-grandmother when the single Jeffry pharmacy was about to file for bankruptcy. They'd extended all around Chicago over the years, and she'd been able to pay for the kids' colleges as the Jeffry's business spread. Now there were two more nearly ready to open in a pricey neighborhood in St. Louis and another in Indianapolis. She could afford to make Mel his own office.

What a good wedding present that would be? It couldn't be a surprise, however. He'd want to be involved. And he could figure where the windows would be, where to put his files, the desk and chair, and the old cowboy lamp he's had as a boy.

While Jane was planning all she had to do before the wedding, she and Shelley went to take their first class in Women's Safety. On the way, Jane said,

"I emailed my dad that I was going to marry Mel and wanted them here. He emailed back, 'Please tell me you're not pregnant.' He has a good sense of humor—he thinks."

Most of the class had already assembled. There were only seven of them tonight. The leader called them to attention. She was something of a surprise. She looked to be around fifty years of age, but Mel had referred to her as an old lady.

Jane whispered this fact to Shelley. "We're getting closer to being fifty ourselves."

"Never say that again," Shelley snapped. "She must be older than we think. Lots of plastic surgery until you look at the turkey skin of her throat."

"I'm Miss Elinor Brooker Welborne. And never call me 'Ms.'" Let's get your first names sorted out. Everyone obeyed in turn. Except the youngest, a girl of about twenty who was dressed in a long-sleeved blouse and jeans. She said she was Sara Tokay.

"All right. Show me your purses before we begin."

An odd request, Jane thought, but they all obediently obeyed.

"Jane has the best. But you kept it under your chair. Don't ever do that again."

"Why?" Jane asked boldly.

"Because it's dangerous. Anybody behind you could have hooked it with their foot and gone through it."

This remark resulted in some outraged muttering.

"Purses are important. Jane's has a long strap. But she should wear it over her opposite shoulder and in front of her. Purse snatchers would be glad to take any of the other purses the rest of you brought with you."

She went on, "I have the names of two cobblers in Chicago who could install a flexible steel wire in the strap, so purse snatchers couldn't cut through it with a sharp knife or box cutter. I'll give you their names and addresses at the end of this session."

"That's interesting," Shelley whispered to Jane.

Miss Welborne went on to explain about pick pockets. She said to always buy trousers, skirts and jackets with pockets, preferably with button closures, and put your cash and one credit card in one pocket. Leave the other credit cards behind in a safe place at home. Also put your driver's license in your front pocket. And never put a house key in your handbag or billfold. She suggested as well that women who operated on largely a cash basis, only take along with you to the grocery store or a shop what they could afford to lose.

"Leave the rest of your cash at home, well hidden."

Jane was sitting next to Shelley with Sara Tokay on her other side.

Sarah pushed her sleeve back to look at her wristwatch.

"This is enough for you to absorb in this first meeting. We'll get together and go over other matters on Thursday evening.

Jane was doing as she'd been told, holding her purse in front of her, passing the strap over one shoulder and under and front of the other arm.

"That was good advice," she said as she hauled herself up into Shelley's minivan. Did you see that young girl's arm when she looked at her wristwatch?"

"I didn't notice that she did that. Why do you ask?" Shelley asked, shoving the car into drive and shooting out the parking lot at a furious rate. Jane, as always, had her foot firmly on the nonexistent brake peddle on the passenger side.

"Because the girl had a terrible bruise on her arm."

That's a bit alarming. But maybe she was careless and got it herself," Shelley said, taking a sharp right turn that felt as if she'd done it on only the right wheels.

"Maybe. Or maybe not," Jane said.